Was he a brute? O

His skin was tanned to the color of her leather saddle, his chest and back, as well. And he wore no drawers…!

An irrational thought flicked through her mind. Could a man's backside get suntanned right through his jeans?

A brute, she decided. A man who chases others for money. A bounty hunter who would turn in his own father for a price. Hardheaded and hard-hearted.

Then why did he want to save his prisoner's life?

She could feel him staring at her, asking a silent question. It took all her courage to meet his gaze. His eyes were hard. Calculating. And unusual.

There was something undisciplined about him. Primitive, like a wild animal. A wolf, that was it. A hungry wolf. One who hunted alone.

It didn't exactly make him unacceptable. It made him…*dangerous…!*

* * *

High Country Hero
Harlequin Historical #706—May 2004

Acclaim for Lynna Banning

"Do not read Lynna Banning expecting some trite, clichéd western romance. This author breathes fresh air into the West.
—*Romance Reviews*

The Scout
"Though a romance through and through, *The Scout* is also a story with powerful undertones of sacrifice and longing."
—*Romantic Times*

The Angel of Devil's Camp
"This sweet charmer of an Americana romance has just the right amount of humor, poignancy and a cast of quirky characters."
—*Romantic Times*

The Law and Miss Hardisson
"…fresh and charming…a sweet and funny yet poignant story."
—*Romantic Times*

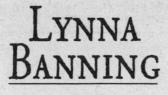

LYNNA BANNING

High Country Hero

HARLEQUIN®

TORONTO • NEW YORK • LONDON
AMSTERDAM • PARIS • SYDNEY • HAMBURG
STOCKHOLM • ATHENS • TOKYO • MILAN • MADRID
PRAGUE • WARSAW • BUDAPEST • AUCKLAND

ISBN 0-373-29306-2

HIGH COUNTRY HERO

Copyright © 2004 by The Woolston Family Trust

This edition published by arrangement with Harlequin Books S.A.

www.eHarlequin.com

Printed in U.S.A.

Please address questions and book requests to:
Harlequin Reader Service
U.S.: 3010 Walden Ave., P.O. Box 1325, Buffalo, NY 14269
Canadian: P.O. Box 609, Fort Erie, Ont. L2A 5X3

For my niece, Leslie Yarnes Sugai.

With grateful thanks to Suzanne Barrett,
Kathleen Dougherty, Susan Renison, Tricia Adams,
Bonnie Hamre, Brenda Preston, Carol Crosby
and David Woolston.

Chapter One

Russell's Landing, Oregon
1884

The instant Sage turned the corner onto Main Street, she saw the woman in purple calico barreling down the board sidewalk toward her. Oh, no. Not Mrs. Benbow. The plump seamstress was the biggest busybody in town.

Sage stopped, smiled and prepared to have her ears burned by the latest gossip.

"Ain't seen it yet, have ya, honey?"

"Seen what?"

"Why, the newspaper, of course. The *Willamette Valley Voice*. My stars, that man has a tongue somewhere's between a rattlesnake and a grizzly bear."

"Mr. Stryker, you mean?"

"Who else?" Nelda Benbow's voice was sharp with gleeful outrage. "That man gets the whole town in an uproar every single Thursday. Mind you, I don't think he really believes half the things he publishes in that puffed-up rag of his, but the harm's done soon as the ink's dry. And the hurt," she added in a gentler tone. She sent Sage a pitying look.

"Hurt," Sage echoed. "Who has Mr. Stryker crucified this time?"

"Best you set down afore you read it, Sage dear."

The older woman gave her a quick pat on the shoulder and sped on down the walkway toward Duquette's Mercantile.

It? What "it"?

Sage had troubles enough without worrying over who Mr. Stryker's latest victim was. Last Thursday it had been Miles Schutte, head of the school board. In an editorial entitled The Three R's—Rum-soaked, Ridiculous and Rabble-rousing, the newspaper editor had lambasted Mr. Schutte with a stream of inflammatory adjectives and innuendo, all because he had drunk a toast at the school board meeting in honor of the new teacher, Miss Euphemia Prescott. Last year's schoolmarm, Molly Landon, had gotten married in the spring, and married women weren't allowed to teach in Douglas County.

Or anywhere else in Oregon, as far as Sage knew. The restriction was positively medieval. One would think mankind would be more enlightened near the end of the nineteenth century.

Perhaps Mr. Stryker would address this inequity? Her neatly buttoned shoes carried her straight to the newspaper office.

At her entrance, the editor rose to his feet. "Good morning, Miss West. Oh, I beg your pardon. *Dr.* West."

A thrill of pure pride shot through her. *Dr. Sage West.* It had taken her six grueling years, and she wanted everyone in town to celebrate her accomplishment. For the first time since its founding, Russell's Landing had a physician.

"Mr. Stryker." She smiled at the bony, stern-faced man who stood across the polished wood counter from her. He and his wife, Flora, had never had children of their own. When Sage was growing up, Friedrich Stryker had always slipped lemon drops to her when she had come into the newspaper office with her father.

She dug a five-cent piece from her reticule, dropped it on the counter and scanned the front page. Mugwumps Desert Blaine for Cleveland.

Railroad Tunnel Collapses. Republicans Bicker over Tariff.

"Article's on page three," the graying newspaper editor said in a dry voice. "My editorial's on page seven." He pocketed the coin and retreated to his desk.

Sage flipped the paper open and buried her nose in the third page. The still-wet black ink smelled sharp and oily. Engrossed, she moved to the shop entrance, pushed the door open and stepped out onto the boardwalk.

Recently returned from Philadelphia where she completed her medical studies, Miss Sage Martin West, daughter of Mayor William West and his lovely wife, Henrietta...

She stumbled over a loose board on the walkway.

...away in the East for the past five years...

"Six years," she murmured. "Almost seven. Oh, excuse me, Miss Nyland. I didn't see you come out of the mercantile."

"Reading the article about yourself, are you, Sage?"

"Yes. My, it does seem strange, though. As if I'm somebody else!!"

"Come across Friedrich's editorial yet?"

"No, I—"

"Well, don't take it too hard, dear."

Miss Nyland whisked into the millinery shop, where a jaunty straw sun hat with a purple feather hung in the display window. The woman did love her bonnets, Sage remembered. She had worn them even when she taught school, and that was—my gracious!—thirteen years ago! Now Miss Nyland's prize pupil at Grove School was grown up and wearing bonnets herself. Or should be. Absently Sage smoothed her free hand across her bare head.

She shrugged and went on down the street, her eyes glued to the typeset lines.

...Dr. West has opened her new medical practice at the corner of Maple Falls Lane and Cottage Road, next to the old Mc-Connell homestead.

"Yes!" she exulted. She had her own house, her own reception parlor, her own consulting room.

...office hours are from...

Yes. Oh yes. She was a real doctor at last. And she had come home to keep the town she'd grown up in safe from disease and medical disasters.

She gave a little skip, stepped off the boardwalk and turned to the editorial. The warm June breeze rattled the open pages in front of her face, and she gripped them to keep them still without taking her eyes off the print. Halfway across the rutted road, she came to an abrupt stop.

"'Dried up old maid'?" she yelped. "'So plain a man would have to be blind to...'"

Oh!

She wasn't "plain." She was...well, tall. With a high forehead, a nose she'd always wished were a bit shorter, and a mass of hair the color of a muddy horse trough. "But my eyes are nice," she said aloud.

Anyway, what difference did it make what she looked like? She was a good doctor. A *very* good doctor.

"I have studied for years!" she announced to the empty street.

A horse tied up in front of the hotel lifted its head and gazed at her with one large dark eye. "Well, I did," she reiterated. The horse lowered its muzzle into the feed bag lashed to the rail.

Sage moved on across the road, settled herself

in one of the rocking chairs in front of the mercantile and snapped open the newspaper again.

Well. *Well!* "Oh, for pity's sake!"

Women should be wives and mothers…steadfast at the cradle, happy at the hearth.

"Cooks and nursemaids, is that it, Mr. Stryker? Laundresses and seamstresses and teachers, but not physicians?"

Why not?

She rocked furiously back and forth, then jumped to her feet, crumpled the sheets of newsprint into a ball and retraced her steps to the newspaper office as fast as she could. Before she cleared the doorway, words were tumbling past her lips.

"I thought you were my friend, Mr. Stryker! I thought you—"

Friedrich Stryker leaped from his desk chair and backed away.

"—liked me! Believed in me!"

The man looked stricken. "Well, I do, Miss Sage. I do."

"But you don't think I should be a doctor, is that it?"

"Yes, ahem. Exactly my thoughts. You're a woman—"

She gave him no time to finish. "So what if I am female? I want to be a physician, not a nurse. I've wanted to be a physician ever since I was ten years old and my baby brother died. A nurse could not have saved him. A doctor would have known what to do."

"Well, now, Miss Sage, that is partly—"

She pinned him with her oh-yes-I-can look. "You're just like my professors at medical school. 'Take up nursing,' they advised. 'Get married. Bear children.'"

"Miss Sage, don't you aim to get married at all?"

"No, I do not," she snapped. "First of all, nobody has asked to marry me. And even if someone does, I'll turn him down. A doctor, especially a woman doctor, scarcely has time for her own needs, let alone those of a family."

"Well now, that's just my point." His voice was steadier now.

Sage warmed to her subject. "There are women doctors all over this country—in Massachusetts and Indiana and Missouri and even Idaho. Just who do you think you are, telling us what we can and cannot do?"

The editor put a trembling hand to his face. "I—I'm a journalist, Miss, uh, Dr. West."

"Why on earth would you write such claptrap?" she demanded. *And after all those lemon drops…*

A guilty look crossed Mr. Stryker's face. "Newspapers have been selling pretty good lately," he said in a tight voice. "That's why."

"Then this town is more backward than I thought." She heaved the balled-up newspaper across the counter at him, gathered up her peach-sprigged muslin skirt in both hands and exited with as much decorum as she could manage.

The door did not close properly. She reversed direction, reopened it and this time made sure it shut with a satisfying slam.

Outside, she clenched her fists at her sides and began to count. By the time she reached sixty she had stopped shaking and regained power of speech. She walked on past the mercantile and Essie Ramsey's millinery shop, her shoes hitting the boardwalk so hard her feet tingled. The purple-feathered hat beckoned. She rather fancied it. Was it too ostentatious for a country doctor?

A *woman* country doctor? She was the first female physician in the entire county. She had been the only woman enrolled at Western Reserve, and she had graduated at the top of her class. At this moment she felt she could do anything.

She marched into the millinery shop.

Ten minutes later she emerged with the purple-feathered hat securely pinned to her dark hair. It was a badge of sorts, she acknowledged. She was a doctor who could handle scalpels and forceps, and she was a female, and females wore bonnets! She would wear it each and every single day, with pride.

When she reached the end of the boardwalk, she continued along the well-worn path that led down to the river, her muslin skirt brushing the black-eyed Susans bordering the road. Four houses down, she turned onto Maple Falls Lane and headed for the trim white house that served as combination professional office and residence.

A saddled gray horse stood outside the picket fence, nibbling her Belle of Portugal roses.

"Stop that!" she admonished. "Move along now. Shoo!"

The horse, the same one that had eyed her outside the hotel, lifted its head, whickered and went back to the pale pink blooms. Sage stepped up and slapped her reticule against its rump. "Shoo!"

"No use, ma'am," a voice called. "Sugar never moves once I drop the reins."

Sage looked up to see a pair of dusty black leather boots propped on her front porch railing. From behind the boots the voice came again. "Been waiting for you."

"Oh? Do we know each other, Mr.—?"

"We don't."

She leaned to one side, trying to see past the boots. All she could make out was a tanned, angular face and longish dark hair. "Who are you?"

"Name's not going to mean anything to you, ma'am."

"It might. My uncle's the marshal. I read all the Wanted posters."

Sage caught a flicker of something in his eyes, but it was gone in an instant.

"Name's Lawson."

She inclined her head. "Mr. Lawson." She pushed the gate open and stepped inside. "What do you want? Besides my roses, that is." She gestured toward the mare.

"Sign on the fence says Dr. West lives here. That your father?"

"No. My father is the mayor. He lives three miles outside of town. *I* am Dr. West."

Her announcement was met with silence.

The man stood up and descended the four steps to her level. He was tall, a good head taller than she was. Lean and oddly graceful. He moved with a disconcerting sureness, and his boots made absolutely no sound. A prickle went up her backbone.

"Dr. West?" His voice had a determined edge to it. He extended his hand.

"Y-yes," she acknowledged. She waited for more, but he said nothing, just gripped her fingers and held them, waiting. A flame licked where his skin touched hers.

"Mr. Lawson, was there something you wanted?"

He released her hand. "There is, yes. I rode three days to get here."

"Well, you are here now. What is it that you came for?"

"You."

Sage stared at the man, noting the hip-hugging faded blue jeans, the travel-stained tan shirt, the red bandanna looped inside the open neck.

"Me?" She tried to keep the alarm from her voice. "Why?"

"You're the doctor. Leastways, you said you were."

"As a matter of fact, I am the only doctor in town."

"Only one in the county, it would appear."

"Oh, no. Dr. McGlothlin has a practice over in Dixon Creek."

"That's sixty miles from here. Besides, he's not available. Gone to visit his sister in Missouri for the month. That leaves you."

She swallowed in annoyance. "What seems to be the problem, Mr. Lawson?"

"Not my problem, someone else's. Been shot." He moved through the gate and gathered up the horse's reins. "Come on."

Good Lord, her very first case and it had to be a gunshot wound. Such injuries were often fatal because of sepsis.

"Just where is the patient?" she inquired.

"Three days ride north. You got a saddle horse?"

Three days! "I—no, I don't have a horse. I've only just arrived from the East. I planned to rent a buggy from the livery to make my calls."

"You'll need a horse, not a buggy. Mount behind me and we'll go get you one."

"I will do no such thing! Just who do you think you are, ordering me about?"

He leveled a look at her that made her cold all over. His eyes were an odd gray-green, and hard, like jade. "I'm a man who needs a doctor."

"Well, I cannot just traipse off with you. To begin with, it would cause a scandal, and besides, I have duties to attend to, patients…."

He swung into the saddle and gazed down on her without smiling. "I'll bet you haven't had a single patient since you hung that brand-new shingle on your fence."

Speechless, she gaped at him. She would never, never admit that he was correct. In the fourteen days since she had moved into her new house and opened her medical practice, not one person had sought out her services. Not even Ruth Ollesen, who just three nights ago had delivered her third baby with the help of only her mother, Clara Ramsey, and her sister Essie.

"Get your medical bag," he ordered.

"Now?"

"Now. You can ride double with me, or you can arrange for a horse at the livery. Either way, it's now."

"But—are we going… I mean, alone? Just the two of us?"

"Miss West, I suggest that unless you want to lose your first patient, you get moving."

Sage drew in a breath to the count of five. She couldn't refuse. She had taken an oath to serve when called upon. It would be far worse to let someone die than risk being the butt of Mrs.

Benbow's busy tongue or Friedrich Stryker's newspaper editorials.

"What about—?"

"Whatever is on your mind, we'll talk about it on the trail."

Chapter Two

Cord stared at the young woman when she marched back out of the house. She could scramble when she wanted to. One minute she was swishing through her front gate looking custard-soft in a ruffled pastel dress, the next she was striding down her porch steps in a newfangled skirt split up the middle, a red-plaid flannel shirt two sizes too big for her, and what looked like brand-new shiny boots. Her hair was hidden under a battered gray Stetson with a godawful purple feather stuck in the band, and she lugged a bulky black leather bag in one hand. Under one arm she'd squashed a thick-looking bedroll and a black rain poncho.

"That all you're taking?"

"You said five minutes, Mr. Lawson. This is

the best I could do in the allotted time. I trust *you* are taking care of the meals.''

It wasn't a question, so he didn't answer it.

She shoved the black bag and the bedroll into his lap, stuck her foot on top of his and swung up behind him. ''The livery's at the other end of town. I'll want my own mount.''

''That figures,'' he breathed. He flapped the reins and the horse stepped forward. ''Probably too ladyfied to ride double,'' he muttered under his breath.

''Mr. Lawson, I have very acute hearing. I am not too 'ladyfied' to do anything that is required.''

''Yes, ma'am.''

''I will want to select my own horse.''

''Yes, ma'am,'' he said again.

''There's the livery. Just past the barbershop. Do you see it?''

''Yes, ma'am.''

''A spunky little mare, I think. Something with spirit.''

''No, ma'am. You get something slow and surefooted, like a mule. Trail's treacherous in places.''

''Oh.'' Disappointment sounded in her voice. ''I do not like mules. I prefer horses.''

He guided his mare past the barbershop and

turned in to a well-kept livery yard. "Mules can carry more."

"With only five minutes to pack my things, there's not much that needs carrying."

"Suit yourself. Just remember I warned you." He reined in and she slid backward off the horse's rump. The look on her face made him chuckle. Her wide mouth was pinched, as if she'd bit into a sour lemon, and her blue-violet eyes snapped with indignation. She could hustle when she had to, but she liked having her own way.

Cord made it a point to figure out how a trail companion's mind worked; it spared arguments and allowed him to keep one jump ahead, no matter what. He'd ridden with some humdingers in the past. He'd learned the hard way what being on the trail could do to an otherwise civilized relationship.

"Arvo," she called to the stocky older man who strode toward them. "This is Mr. Lawson."

Cord tipped his hat at the man's nod.

"Vat I can do for you, Mr. Lawson?"

"Lady needs a horse. One that—"

"One that's surefooted and steady," she interrupted. "But not dull, Arvo. There's nothing I hate worse than riding a horse with no intelligence."

"Sure t'ing, Miss Sage. Maybe Ginger or Lightfoot. How far you going?"

"Into the Bear Wilderness area," Cord answered. He watched the liveryman's thick eyebrows jump. "Be gone ten, maybe twelve days."

"Ginger, then. She got better wind for a long trip." The liveryman gave Cord a thoughtful look. "Miss Sage, does your pa know you're going up into the wilderness?"

"Not yet, Arvo. I thought maybe you could ride out and tell him. Tell Papa I've gone to answer a medical call with Mr. Lawson."

"Cordell Lawson," Cord interjected. "The marshal will have heard of me."

Arvo's eyebrows jumped again.

"Don't tell Mama, Arvo. Please. She'll worry herself into a conniption fit. Just Papa."

The liveryman disappeared into the stable, reemerging a few moments later leading a shiny roan mare. "I put your old saddle on her, Miss Sage. You t'ink you remember how to ride?"

She laughed. "I'm not likely to forget how, even if it has been six years since I've sat a horse. Back in Philadelphia it was the one thing I missed more than Papa's apple pancakes."

She busied herself lashing the medical bag and bedroll behind the saddle while Arvo adjusted the stirrups. She was poised to mount when Arvo said, "Vait one minute." He stepped into the stable again and reemerged with a bulky tan garment in his hand.

"My old riding jacket!" Sage reached for it, buried her nose in the soft sheepskin lining. "Smells like horses!" Her delight made Cord want to laugh.

"I keep it nice for you, for when you come back." The older man made a step out of his laced fingers, and Sage swung herself up on the mare. Then she leaned down and hugged him. "Thank you, Arvo. Thank you for believing that I *would* come back. Mama cried and cried, thinking she would never see me again."

"I allus know you vill come back, Miss Sage. Cal, he said you'd marry some back East man vat talks funny, but I know better." He tapped his forehead. "I t'ink to myself that daughter of Billy West and your pretty mama never be happy anywhere but here."

Cord noticed that she waved until she could no longer see the liveryman. It was obvious they were friends. She was known here. Respected. Even loved.

He scanned the length of the main street. Hotel, newspaper office, mercantile, saloon, marshal's office. Nice little town, the kind where everybody knew everybody else, where kids grew up together and got married and raised kids themselves.

He tried to swallow, but something hard was stuck in his throat.

Before they had traveled three-quarters of a mile, Sage decided she didn't like him. He set a pace she couldn't match, and then he leaned back in the saddle and tipped his face into the breeze as if he'd never smelled wild honeysuckle before. As if he'd been starving and here was nourishment in the scent of the air. He stayed that way, looking as if he hadn't a care in the world, while she pushed her mount to keep up.

She rode well. Her father had put her up on a pony before she was out of pinafores, and when she could jump three flour barrels without losing her seat, he taught her Indian tricks. How to grip with her knees and fire a rifle at a dead run. How to swing sideways out of the saddle and snatch up a hat off the ground.

She sucked her breath in and wished she could stop to rest, just for a minute. When she realized she couldn't, at least not without losing her guide, she blew the air out and straightened her shoulders. What she needed on this trip was not

Indian tricks but stamina. Could she be getting soft at twenty-five?

How could he ride that way, sitting the dark mare in that slouched, lazy manner, one hand resting on his thigh, the other holding the reins so loosely the leather barely moved? She'd laugh if a prairie dog spooked his horse; he'd topple off in one second flat. She kept her eye on him. If it happened, she didn't want to miss it.

For the next four hours their route followed the west bank of the Umpqua as it looped and curved its way around stands of Douglas fir and house-high piles of granite boulders. She knew the river, loved every inch of its swift-flowing, emerald waters. She'd learned to swim near her uncle John's place, where the river slowed and widened to lap a sandy beach.

She never liked swimming much. She preferred wading in the shallows, where she could see the stones on the river bottom and knew exactly where to place her feet.

Her mouth felt dry as a dish towel and tasted the same. Would that man never slow down? She was panting for breath, her mouth open; by nightfall her teeth would be black with trail dust.

Nightfall? She eyed the sun, just tipping behind the treetops on the ridge ahead of them. She'd never make it till nightfall.

"Mr. Lawson?" she gasped.

He twisted to look back at her but kept his horse moving.

Oh, the devil with the man! She reined in, brought the mare to a stop and reached for her canteen. She'd downed a single swallow of water when it was wrenched out of her grasp.

"You stop when I stop. Drink when I drink. Someone who's been shot might not have much time."

"I am going as fast as I can." She'd like to fling the contents of the canteen in his face, but she'd be thirsty later if she did. Blast the man. The worst part of it was that he was right—a person with a bullet wound was looking death in the face.

He screwed the cap back on and handed over the container. "Let's ride."

Well, of all the... What if she had to urinate? Would he stride back into the bushes and yank up her drawers? The thought was so bizarre she laughed out loud.

He turned in the saddle and pinned her with a questioning look in those hard, gray-green eyes.

"It's nothing," she said quickly.

But what if her bladder were ready to burst? What would she have to do to make him stop?

She kneed the horse forward and studied the man's back. Cordell Lawson wasn't as easy-going as he appeared. He was driving himself hard and dragging her along with him. Her thighs burned. Her neck hurt from tipping her head against the sun. This was, she realized, a perfect example of mismatched traveling companions. She was human, and he was not.

The trail narrowed and began to climb. Halfway up the steep path she knew she couldn't make it. Rocks jutted above her, and below, the river glinted silver. If the horse stumbled...

She drew rein and stopped.

Cord heard the horse's steps cease. What now? He kept on, hoping she would resume her pace, but no sound came from behind him. Clenching his teeth, he turned his mount.

She had halted in the middle of the trail and was sitting there, slumped in the saddle, with that ridiculous feather drooped over her face. But her hands told him all he needed to know. She wore deerskin riding gloves, and while he couldn't see her knuckles, he knew from the way she gripped the saddle horn that her hands would ache come sundown. Especially if she hadn't sat a horse in—what had she said?—six years. And they'd been on the trail for a full seven hours. Hell, she wouldn't be able to sit down for a week.

Of all the doctors in Oregon, why did he have to find her? She was prim and proper and saddle-green. Too slim and willowy to be very strong. And female. Very definitely female—moods and all. Probably enjoyed herself only once a year, at Christmas.

He'd bet she'd never taken a bath in the woods, either. In two days she'd smell like a rotting cabbage. If there was one thing that spoiled the pleasure of the mountains and the sky and the sweet, fresh air it was a partner who smelled bad.

For a long minute he sat still and watched her. Just when he thought maybe he ought to say something, she kicked her mare and it jolted forward.

She moved toward him, still bent over the saddle horn, her head down, not even watching where she was going. Her shoulders were hunched tight with exhaustion.

But she was moving. She had sand; he'd say that for her.

Chapter Three

Cord watched the exhausted woman pry her fingers off the saddle horn and lay the mare's leather reins in her lap. For the last three hours, as they'd climbed the slope to where the trail leveled off at Frog Jump Butte, she'd hung on by sheer force of will, and her face showed it. Beneath the brim of that sad-looking gray felt hat her eyelids were almost shut.

He let loose an irrepressible snort. No wonder. She was fighting to stay awake, clinging to the hard leather pommel like she'd been glued there.

"Let's make camp," he called.

There was no response.

He dismounted and peered through the darkness at her form, still hunched so low in the saddle the purple feather in her hatband brushed the mare's ear.

"You all right?" he ventured.

After a long silence, a gravelly voice drifted out of the shadows. "Do you always travel like this? Of course I am not all right. I'm half-dead."

"Travel like what? You're not half-dead. You can still talk, can'tcha? I hate a woman who exaggerates."

She straightened, groaned and tried to swing her leg over the horse's back to dismount. "I know your friend is in need of medical help, but you travel like someone is breathing down your neck."

She gave up, hefted her bottom over the cantle and slid off the mare backward. When her feet hit the ground, she grasped the animal's tail to keep from staggering and leaned her forehead against the mare's hindquarters.

"Maybe someone is," he said.

She just shook her head and made a small moaning noise.

Goddamn, was she crying? "I'll build a fire."

She lifted her head and took a wobbly step. "I would gather some kindling for you, Mr. Lawson, but I don't think I can bend over. Who would be following you?"

He didn't answer. Five minutes of scrounging and his arms were full of pinecones and dry branches. He kicked some rocks into a circle and dumped his load. As far as he could tell, she hadn't moved.

"You can stand up all night if you want, Doc, but I wouldn't advise it."

"I will be seated when I am…able. In the meantime, I need to answer a call of nature." She took another shaky step and grabbed the horse's tail again.

Cord tossed three broken tree limbs onto his unlit fire and strode toward her. "If you were a man, you could pee right where you're standing. Seeing as you're not…"

He grasped her elbows and propelled her ahead of him into the scrub. "See that big huckleberry bush? Use that."

He released her, and she swayed forward.

"Yes," she murmured. "Thank you. I can manage now."

He tramped back to the fire pit while she made rustling sounds in the brush. Out of courtesy he decided not to ignite the kindling until she'd finished. Firelight would illuminate the whole area.

He waited, stalked off into the woods on the other side of camp to do his own business, then squatted beside the fire and waited some more, his flint box poised and ready.

Nothing. Not one leaf rattle or scritch-scratch

of twigs came from the direction of the huckleberry bush. An evening songbird started in, stopped, then resumed singing. What in blazes was taking her so long?

"Dr. West?"

There was no answer.

She couldn't have stumbled off the edge of the butte. Hell's bells, she couldn't walk that far. What was she doing?

"Dr. West? Sage?"

To heck with her. He struck a spark and puffed his breath onto the thatch of smoldering pine needles. When it caught, he added more branches, then unloaded his saddlebag.

As he worked laying out his bedroll and the supper things, he listened.

The sparrow twittered on as if it was his last night on earth. A coyote yipped somewhere. But nothing sounded like a female doing her business behind a bush. He began to wonder about that split-up-the-front skirt she wore. Did it unbutton between her legs? Or did she have to pull it down and drop her drawers? Anatomically, women were at a disadvantage.

The songbird stopped abruptly, after which he heard nothing but the occasional spark popping from the fire. What in blazes was going on behind that huckleberry bush? Nobody took half an hour to pee.

"Sage?" He stood up. "Dr. West? I'm coming over." His boots crunched through the bracken, managing to stop just before he tripped over her.

She lay curled up on her side, her hat squashed into the pine needles. Cord knelt beside her, checked her breathing.

Sound asleep. He suppressed a chuckle. Just one tuckered out, ladyfied lady. He'd bet she'd pulled up her drawers and then just fallen over.

Oh, boy. He'd have to wake her up for supper.

He strode back to camp, untied her bedroll and spread it out by the fire. He mixed up some biscuits, then opened a tin of beans and set it on a flat rock. Over it, close to the heat, he placed the tin pan with six lumps of sticky biscuit dough arranged in a circle, and one in the middle. No fresh water up here, so they'd make do with what was left in the canteens.

And whiskey. His mouth watered at the thought. He wouldn't get drunk, just smooth out the rough places. It had been a long time since he'd felt this edgy.

She was still asleep when he went to get her. "Doc?" He nudged her shoulder with the toe of his boot. "Wake up. Supper's ready."

She groaned and pulled her knees up closer to her chin.

"Doc?" Aw, the devil with it. He went down on one knee, slid his arms under her and stood up. She weighed no more than a sack of sugar. Her long legs swung as he moved, but she didn't wake up.

He laid her out on her bedroll and she opened her eyes and looked up at him. "Just what do you think you are doing, manhandling my person?"

Man, did she wake up fast! Her voice was clear as a cold creek.

"You fell asleep. I lugged you out of the woods for supper."

She sat up. "Supper?"

"Beans and biscuits." And whiskey.

"Oh?" She smiled and her whole face lit up, especially her eyes. In the firelight they looked like the purple pansies Nita used to grow. Big and velvety.

"You haven't answered my question," Sage said.

"Huh? What question?"

"Who is following us?"

Cord sent her a sharp look. A more single-minded female he'd never encountered. He thought he'd sidestepped the issue hours ago. "Nobody's following us," he said quickly.

"I don't believe you."

He leaned back and stared at her. "You know, I had a dog like you once. Used to get his teeth into something and wouldn't let go."

"I had a dog like you once, too," she said with a sideways look. "He used to drop a ham bone at my feet and then bite me if I picked it up."

Cord sat back on his heels and studied her. High cheekbones. Three or four freckles. A generous mouth, still rosy from sleep. Kind of an English nose. And those eyes. She was pretty, but too smart for her own good.

He switched tactics. "You like venison in your beans?"

"Is your real name Cordell?"

"What's that got to do with it?"

She gave him a tired smile. "Nothing. I just wanted you to know I could do it, too."

"Do what, cook?"

"No." She looked straight into his eyes. "Change subjects when I need to."

Oh, yeah. Sand and then some.

Sage eyed the pocketknife he slipped out of his jeans. He snapped it open with a flick of his long fingers, and she caught her breath. It looked as sharp as any scalpel she'd ever picked up, and when he pulled a leathery-looking strip of dried jerky from a dingy flour sack and carved off two-bit-size rounds, she began to breathe again. He grinned at her as if he knew what she'd been thinking and dropped them into the tin of bubbling beans.

"Is that knife really clean?" she said without thinking.

"Clean enough," he responded.

"But we're going to eat that! What about bacteria? Germs?"

"What about 'em? The heat'll kill the puny ones, and this—" he dribbled in a healthy splash of whiskey "—will make the survivors happy."

"I wasn't thinking about the survivors. I was thinking about the *ingesters*." She used the word on purpose.

"We'll live."

"And the germs won't."

"Life's like that. Germ eat germ, so to speak. What are you so touchy about, Doc? You're gettin' your supper cooked, your toes toasted by the fire I built, everything but tucked in with a bedtime story."

"I know." She sighed. "I am grateful, Mr. Lawson. Tomorrow I won't be so worn-out."

"Sure you won't," he said dryly. "Here. Eat

up.'' He handed her a fork and a tin plate swimming with hot beans, topped by two overbrowned biscuits. She stabbed one with her fork, but it slid sideways. She grabbed it with her fingers and bit into a corner. Or tried to.

"Who in the world taught you how to make biscuits?"

He shoveled a load of beans into his mouth. "Zack Beeler."

Her fork clattered onto the plate. "*The* Zack Beeler?"

Cord's black eyebrows rose a fraction of an inch. "You heard of him?"

"Everyone's heard of him. He's an outlaw! A bank robber and a murderer. I saw his poster in my uncle's office when I was just a girl."

"He's also a fine trail cook. He taught me to make biscuits when I was seven."

Sage stared at Cord. *Just what kind of man was he?* "Mr. Lawson, what is it you do for a living?"

"I'm a bounty hunter."

Oh. *Oh.* "Is the individual who needs a doctor, um…*wanted?*"

"You could say that." He dribbled a tablespoon of whiskey over his beans. "In a manner of speaking."

Speechless, Sage watched him smash up his

biscuits with the fork tines and scoop beans over them. *An outlaw.* She was struggling up this trail to treat someone from the shady side of the law? Someone who might possibly be—in fact, likely was—dangerous?

"Is this person your prisoner?"

"Not exactly. Close enough, though. Can't move much with a bullet in the back."

She picked up her fork, then set it down. She had to eat, had to keep up her strength. But suddenly the thought of beans and biscuits lost its appeal.

He cocked his head at her. "Something the matter?"

"Not hungry."

"Scared, you mean."

"Don't put words in my mouth, Mr. Lawson."

"Better put some beans in it, then. Long day tomorrow. You don't eat, you won't be much good."

She sat back and digested his words, watching his hand move methodically from the plate in his lap to his mouth and back. She could deal with this, couldn't she? Deal with him? A man she'd known a mere twelve hours? Scramble after him on a barely visible trail into the wilderness to treat Lord only knew who?

She set her plate of food on the ground beside her and tipped sideways until her shoulder met the bedroll, then drew her knees up, wrapped her arms over her stomach and shut her eyes.

His voice came from across the fire pit. "I know it's tough. Hard riding when you haven't sat a horse in some years. Steep trail. The river yet to cross."

Her heart leaped. *Cross the river? Would she have to swim?*

"Maybe you're afraid you're not going to measure up?"

"I'll measure up, Mr. Lawson." She licked her lips. "But…would it be all right if I measured up tomorrow?"

The last thing she heard was the clink of tinware and his low chuckle.

Chapter Four

The next morning, Cord lay in his blanket, purposely not moving any part of his body, especially his head. How much had he drunk last night—a third of his stash? Half? He'd lay off when he'd got the doc up the mountain. In the meantime, he'd kill the thing that weighed on him any way he could.

He heard noises around the camp, but his eyes wouldn't open. "What time is it?"

"Morning," a female voice said. "Almost."

He cracked one eyelid. "What are you doing up so damn early?"

"I am 'measuring up,' Mr. Lawson." She waved a pan of fluffy-looking mounds under his nose. "Now *these*," she announced with a note of satisfaction, "are biscuits."

He inhaled and had to agree; they sure smelled like biscuits.

"Get up, and you can have some."

He drew in another breath and smelled bacon. And coffee. *Oh, yes, Lord. Coffee.* Measuring up? Hell's bells, she was saving his life!

He watched her move back to the campfire.

She seemed stiff. He noticed she didn't bend over, just flexed her knees to reach down. He wondered how she'd managed to poke the coals into a cookfire.

She dipped, straight-backed, and turned over the sizzling bacon strips with a fork. The coffee simmered in the bean tin from last night's supper.

"I see you found the supplies."

"And your revolver," she said in a neutral tone. "And your whiskey. Quite a lot of whiskey, in fact."

Cord's breath hissed in. "Didn't pour it out, did you?" That's all he needed, a temperance advocate on a cross-country ride.

"Certainly not. Whiskey is an excellent disinfectant."

He rolled out from under the scratchy, army-issue blanket and stood up. Mistake. He shut his eyes against the pounding in his temples and dropped to his knees. Lord God, he'd done it again.

"Here." Her voice came from somewhere close by, and the next thing he knew she was folding his fingers around a tin mug. "Drink it," she ordered. "And don't vomit."

His stomach flipped at the word. *I won't. I can't. Not with her watching.* He brought the mug to his nose and inhaled. She might be a prim and proper lady, but she sure could make coffee. He slurped in a mouthful. She measured up just fine.

"Ready for breakfast?"

"No," he growled.

"Your boots are warming by the fire."

"Thanks."

"Your shirt's airing out on that tree limb."

"Airing out?"

"It's filthy," she said, her voice crisp.

"*I'm* filthy. Haven't had a bath since—"

She tsk-tsked. "Inadequate hygiene. We'll bathe tonight. Assuming we camp near a stream."

Cord let a long minute pass while he sipped hot coffee and tested his equilibrium.

"And another thing," she began. "I do not think—"

"Hold it," he snapped. He lifted his free hand

toward her, fingers up. "Hold it right there. You sure as hell are measuring up. Any more and I'll have to hand over my pants and let you wear 'em."

"Well, that won't be necessary I'm sure, Mr. Lawson." She sounded pleased. "But now that you mention it, since you are wearing your pants, would you mind putting on the rest of your clothes before we eat? I am not used to sharing my meals with a half-dressed gentleman."

"I don't much care what you're used to, Doc. And as for the gentleman part—"

"You needn't explain," she said, her voice matter-of-fact. "I am aware."

Cord stalked over to the fire and stuffed his right foot into his boot. "Ouch! Goldarnit, it's hot!"

Her eyes widened. "Don't you wear socks?"

"Did you find any socks when you rustled through my things?" he growled.

"No. But I sleep with mine on, so I naturally thought…"

Cord glared at her. "Well, I sleep with mine off. In fact, I never wear socks. Or drawers, so don't yank my pants off cuz you think they need 'airing.'"

"Which they do," she offered. There was a

hint of laughter in her voice, but he was too mad—and too hungry, he realized—to care.

''My pants,'' he said with as much dignity as he could muster, ''don't get washed until they need it, and that's not until they can stand up by themselves.''

''Well, then. If the knees will still bend, perhaps you would like to sit down and eat some breakfast.''

It wasn't a question, more like a softly spoken order, but the grumbling of his stomach made a response irrelevant. Jupiter, could she get under his skin! He noticed that she ate standing up.

The crisp bacon broke up in his mouth like little shards of sweet-flavored cookies, and the biscuits! Fluffy white tumbleweeds that melted on his tongue. He swallowed and nearly groaned with pleasure. ''Who taught *you* to cook?''

''Billy West. He's my father.''

Cord stopped chewing. ''I don't know who my father is. Could have been any one of four men, all of 'em outlaws.''

''Outlaws?''

''Only family I ever knew. My mother died having me. They fed me and clothed me until I was fifteen.''

''And then?''

His face changed. ''And then I turned them

in. They'd killed a Chinese woman and her baby."

Sage opened her mouth to speak, then thought better of it. What brutes men could be. Some men, anyway. Her father and Uncle John were both wonderful men, strong and smart and gentle inside, where it counted.

She glanced at the man seated on the other side of the fire. *What about him?* A brute? Or a gentle man?

A dark whisker shadow lay over the lower half of his face. His skin was tanned the color of her leather saddle, his chest and back, as well. And he wore no drawers.

An irrational thought flicked through her mind. Could a man's backside get suntanned right through his jeans?

He was a brute, she decided. A man who chased other men for money. A bounty hunter who would turn in his own father for a price. Hardheaded and hard-hearted.

Then why did he want to save his prisoner's life?

She could feel him staring at her, asking a silent question. It took all her courage to meet his gaze. His eyes were hard. Calculating. And unusual. The gray-green irises were ringed with brown, as if they had started to be one color in utero and then changed to another before birth.

There was something undisciplined about him. Primitive, like a wild animal. A wolf—that was it. A hungry wolf. One who hunted alone.

She dropped her gaze to the tin plate in her hand. That fact didn't exactly make him unacceptable. It made him dangerous.

Three switchbacks down Frog Jump Butte it started to rain. The cold, stinging droplets dampened the trail, then turned it into mud. The horses twitched their tails and stepped daintily along the precipitous cliff edge while Sage's heart thumped.

She'd packed into the woods before with her father and Uncle John, but if it rained, the three of them would hole up in a cave or a tree hollow and wait it out. Camping trips when she was a girl had been for fun.

Now she was "all growed up" as her father put it, and it wasn't fun. Not with rainwater sluicing off her hat and a sopping wet riding skirt clinging to her legs. The brown denim material made a *swish-slap* sound with every step the horse took.

As the morning wore on, the sky grew darker. Rain dribbled in rivulets off the toes of her boots, splashed onto the ground and made the already sodden trail even more slippery. She reached one gloved hand to pat the mare's neck. "Good girl," she murmured. "We will soldier on."

Sage had picked up the phrase from her father, had used it at medical college when things had seemed insurmountable—dissecting her first cadaver under the eagle eye of three professors ready to pounce on a false move; fending off the rude, hurtful jests by her male colleagues when a patient happened to be female; even forcing herself to eat when she was so tired just opening her mouth took more energy than she could muster.

She had soldiered on. Hour by hour, day by day. More than her examinations and flawless oral presentations, her medical degree had come through dogged perseverance.

A little thing like rain might be cold and wet and uncomfortable, but it wouldn't stop her.

But the river, when they reached it, did. It rippled deep green and turquoise around a cluster of water-smoothed gray boulders and a half-submerged fir stump.

"Why," she said to the man who drew rein at her side, "did we climb up that butte yesterday only to unclimb it today? Why not just go *around* it?"

He studied the riverbank, the waterlogged tree, then the opposite bank. "Because you can see the whole valley from up there."

"And be seen, as well."

He hesitated. "True."

He dismounted and shucked off his poncho. "River won't be this smooth for long. It'll rise with the creek runoff." He began to unbutton his shirt.

"What are you doing?"

"Going swimming." He pulled off his boots, rolled them up inside his shirt and poncho and tied them behind the saddle. Raindrops rolled down his bare chest and back.

"Now? In the rain?"

He flashed her a grin. "If you've never gone swimming in the rain, you ought to try it. Rain makes the water seem warm, feels good against your skin. Like silk."

He slapped the mare's rump. "Come on, Sugar." When the horse jolted forward, he splashed into the river alongside her.

Sage watched his half-clothed body slice through the water. Halfway across he rolled onto his back, stretched both arms wide and opened his mouth wide to the rain. "Goddamn, this feels good," he called. "Care to join me?"

She sat frozen on her horse. "What on earth for?" she shouted.

"For pleasure, pure and simple." She thought she heard a low laugh, but she wasn't sure.

"It's one good way to get across the river," he added in a lazy voice. "Besides, my trousers are getting washed at the same time."

Oh, God, the river. She had to cross it, too.

She couldn't swim fully clothed. She'd have to take off her rain gear, then her shirt, her riding skirt. Her boots. She could strip down to her camisole and underdrawers, but he would be watching and...

Does it really feel like silk?

In her entire life, she had never done anything just for pleasure alone. She'd gone camping to learn about medicinal herbs and roots. She'd even kissed a boy once, but only because someone dared her to, and she never backed away from a challenge.

But just to feel...silky? It seemed indecent, somehow. Decadent.

This was crazy. *He* was crazy.

And yet...

Chapter Five

Cord lay spread-eagled in the water, sculling his cupped hands to keep from drifting downstream. He let the raindrops beat on his face and chest as he watched her horse dance back and forth on the sandy riverbank while its rider tried to make up her mind about something. To swim across or ride across, he guessed. Not a big decision; the water was only four, maybe five feet deep.

Swimming in the rain is a real sensual pleasure, Doc. So why not swim across and enjoy the experience? Lord knew there weren't that many real pleasures in this world. When one dropped into your lap, you ought to savor it.

She stepped her mount to the river's edge, studied the wavelets lapping at the mare's hooves, then reined the animal away.

What is she waiting for? The rain had already drenched her; she looked sodden and miserable, with her head down, her shoulders hunched. She was probably shivering so hard her teeth chattered. *Wet is wet, Doc. Choose the way that feels good.*

"Can you swim?" he yelled.

"Yes, I can."

"Well, come on, then."

"I am not familiar with this part of the river. I...don't know if it's safe."

Safe? "Hell, Doc, I'm out here in the middle of it. Doesn't that tell you something?"

"*I* am not *you,* Mr. Lawson. I like to know what is, well, what is beneath the surface before I plunge into something."

"Can't always know that."

"I am r-realizing th-that."

Jehoshaphat, she was so cold she was starting to stutter. "Take a chance, dammit!"

Once more she turned the horse away from the river.

Snakes and sawdust! Maybe she just plain didn't know how to enjoy herself.

But when she turned back, her hand was at her throat, unbuttoning her black rain poncho. Then her red plaid shirt. She dismounted and fumbled at the waistband of her skirt, then stepped out of it and shucked off her boots. Standing there in nothing but her white drawers and a lacy camisole, she looked like a butterfly whose cocoon had just been peeled away.

Cord sucked in a breath. *You see a woman naked and it changes things.* He stopped sculling and let the water close over his head. When he surfaced, she was rolling up her clothes and boots in the poncho. She stashed the bundle behind the saddle, hooked the reins around the pommel and waded into the water. The mare followed at a respectful distance.

Cord wasn't watching the mare. The thin, wet fabric of her underclothes plastered itself to her knees, her thighs. She moved slowly, very slowly, using her arms for balance and testing each step tentatively before she put down her weight. Her body broke the smooth surface with scarcely a ripple. Up to her waist now. Higher, higher…

Oh, hell yes! Under the wet camisole her breasts showed clearly, like mounds of some perfectly formed fruit with a dark aureola marking each center. *Oh, God, she was beautiful.* He couldn't look away.

Then with a splash she was swimming, clean, sharp strokes that cut the water with no noise. A man had taught her, he could see that. Her father, or her uncle, the marshal. At least Cord hoped so. All at once he couldn't stand the thought of another male's hands touching her.

She swam to within a foot of where he lay and, without slowing, glided on past. Her eyes, he noted, were scrunched shut. He rolled onto his stomach and stroked after her.

She reached the sandy beach ahead of him and waded out of the water, her backside gleaming wetly under the clinging muslin. Cord's arms stopped working and he stifled the groan that rose from his belly, a growl of pure male hunger.

And then his sex rose and grew hard.

She caught the mare's bridle as it clambered up the bank, then turned and stood waiting for him, her face composed.

Cord swam into the shallows, but his member was so engorged he didn't dare stand up. Instead, he folded his knees and huddled on the sandy river bottom. He'd have to play for time.

"Enjoy your swim?"

"Yes, I did." She gave him a tentative smile. "I swam all the way across," she said unnecessarily. She beamed like a kid watching a parade, as if she was proud of herself.

What was it she'd said? *I like to know what's beneath the surface before I plunge into some-*

thing. She'd been scared of the river. Scared of the unknown. *Well, I'll be damned.*

Now what?

He waited, up to his neck in the river.

She waited on the bank.

His knees were getting cold. "Want to turn your back while I get out?"

Her eyes flickered. "I'm a doctor, Mr. Lawson. There is nothing about the male body I haven't seen before."

Maybe. Had she ever seen an erection that tented a man's trousers even when they were soaking wet? He didn't think cadavers or ailing male patients could...

"Oh, very well," she said at last. "Since you are shy."

"Shy!" He swooshed to a standing position just in time to see her backside disappear into a gooseberry thicket.

Shy! He glanced down at the front of his jeans. "Sure, Doc. If you say so." He had a hard time keeping a straight face.

To take his mind off the matter, he gathered a handful of pale green gooseberries and fed them to his horse. Slowly.

"Ready to ride?" he called when he thought he was under control.

"Quite ready." She emerged from the thicket

fully dressed, her red shirt buttoned up to her chin, her skirt flaring over her boots. Hell, she looked ready for church.

And here he stood, like a randy cowboy with a hard-on.

The downpour ceased abruptly, as if someone had suddenly turned off a spigot. She glanced skyward, stuck out her hand, palm up. "Oh, look, the rain has stopped. Now my undergarments will dry."

Blazes, she didn't even notice the bulge in his pants! He'd guess she wouldn't understand it if she *did* see it. He rolled his eyes.

She mounted her horse and turned its rump toward him. Clipped to the saddle blanket with four wooden clothespins were her drawers and the lacy camisole.

Cord thought about that as he sloshed out of the river and caught his own mare. Underclothes flapping on the back of her horse. It would be hard not to look at them.

Okey-doke. Then he wouldn't look.

He swung up into the saddle. Water squished out of his wet jeans, coursed down the animal's hide and dripped off the stirrups. Every move he made reminded him he was sodden as a drowning rat.

And hard.

He'd keep his eyes on that funny-looking skirt she wore, and that plaid shirt she'd buttoned up tight like a prissy schoolmarm. He wouldn't think for one second about the fact that she wore absolutely nothing underneath…

Lord-oh-Lord. It was going to be a long, long day.

She rode behind him, had done so ever since they left the Umpqua River three hours ago and headed east cross-country toward the Green Mountains, but it didn't help. He kept thinking about her backside.

He tried reciting multiplication tables in his head. When he completed the twelves, he tried poetry. "This is the forest primeval…"

No good. His now-dry jeans rubbed his flesh the wrong way.

He'd try conversation, he decided. Anything to keep his thoughts from wandering where they had no business going. He twisted in the saddle and spoke over his shoulder. "How come you swim with your eyes closed?"

No answer. After a good dozen heartbeats, her voice floated to him. "Because it scares me."

"But you did it. You looked pretty pleased with yourself after you got across."

"I *was* pleased. Swimming across that river is a milestone for me."

He chuckled. "Like Caesar crossing the Rubicon."

She made a noise somewhere between a cough and a chortle. "How would you know about the Rubicon?"

"I read about it."

"In Latin, I suppose." Her tone indicated disbelief.

"Yeah. Zack Beeler taught me. His mama was a schoolteacher back in Rhode Island. Zack knew more about Latin than making biscuits."

She didn't respond.

"You don't believe me?"

"Let's just say I am...skeptical."

"Try me."

"All right, if you insist. *Caveat viator.*"

"Let the traveler beware," he translated instantly. *"Carpe diem,"* he tossed back.

"Seize the day," she said in a triumphant voice. "So there!" He could tell she was smiling. He wished he could see her face; it lit up when she smiled.

He decided to push his advantage. *"Quam minimum credula postero?"*

"Trust...um, trust..."

"Trust tomorrow as little as possible," he finished for her. "I rest my case."

A long, long silence followed. Cord concentrated on the faint trail ahead of him, noted the angle of the sun, the various shades of green in the wooded area to his right. Pretty country. No settlers. Not even a stage stop out here in the middle of nowhere. It suited him just fine.

When he was tracking someone, he rode through towns, talked to ranchers, stopped at army posts and Indian camps. After a capture he preferred to be alone. Raised by four men on the run, he'd never been comfortable around civilized people. The first Latin word he ever learned was *solus.* Solitary.

Ah, what the hell. People were no damn good anyway.

Except for her, maybe. Most folks pointed fingers, spat out insults, drew sidearms on a fellow for no cause but suspicion or being "different."

She was an exception. She had the gumption to ride with him, and that said quite a lot about her. She was dedicated to her profession.

She was…

Don't think about it, Cord. Don't think about those underclothes, either. Dry by now. Hanging out in plain sight getting bleached by the sun. Probably warm to the touch. She'd slide those drawers up her legs, over her thighs, around her—

"Seven times seven is forty-nine," he said aloud. "'The murmuring pines and the hemlocks...'"

Forget Longfellow. "'I knew a maiden, fair to see...'" He swallowed and dredged up some more Latin from his memory. *"Sic transit gloria mundi."*

Oh, yeah? The glory of the world wasn't passing; it was riding not twenty paces behind him.

"Seven times eight..."

Sage heard him muttering ahead of her, a low rumble that rose and fell like the humming of bees. She couldn't hear distinct words, but maybe that was just as well. What would a man like Cord Lawson, a bounty hunter who spoke Latin of all things, have on his mind?

As she thought about it, the niggle of interest turned into a nagging curiosity. She had always hungered to know what lay beneath the surface of things that were more complex than met the eye; it didn't matter if it was a swollen area of skin on the chest or stomach of a patient, a river, even a whiskery man who swam the dirt out of his laundry. She'd like to peel him open and peer inside.

She watched his bare back moving with the

horse. He must ride shirtless more often than not, she decided. His skin was smooth and very, very tan, so dark it resembled the rich mahogany of her mother's piano. His ear-length black hair had dried in the breeze, and now the ends wanted to curl up. It made him seem young. Even looking into a mirror he wouldn't see how boyish and untamed those little uncorraled strands appeared.

She liked that. It was as if she could see part of him that he himself didn't know existed.

She studied his shoulders, tried to estimate their breadth, then let her gaze drift down his spine to where the subtly moving bones of his back disappeared under the leather belt at his waist. There wasn't an ounce of extra fat on him. Extra anything, really; his torso looked as if it was carved out of dark clay and rubbed smooth with knowing hands.

An odd feeling lodged in her lower belly, as if she had gulped hot chocolate on a winter afternoon. The rich, warm sensation came as a surprise, and she felt it again when he turned to look at her.

"I figure another three hours till we make camp." He squinted against the sun behind her, reached up one hand, pulled his black hat down to his eyebrows. Beneath the tilted brim, his green-gray eyes narrowed.

He was waiting for something, but what? She hadn't requested a necessary stop, or even time to rinse her dry mouth with a bit of water from the canteen. She hadn't slowed him down in the slightest. And after her inquiries about her patient—the location of the wound, the presence of fever and a dozen other questions he had simply sidestepped—she had given up. She prayed that the wounded man would still be alive when they reached him.

She had been an ideal traveling companion, pushing as fast as she could, never complaining. So why was he looking at her like that?

"You all right, Doc?" he called back to her.

"Yes, of course. Why do you ask?"

"Mighty quiet."

"I am…thinking."

He grinned suddenly. "You know, I've about got you figured out." He turned back to scan the trail ahead. The Bear Wilderness area loomed before them, a thick tangle of Douglas fir and spruce that swathed the hills in various shades of brown and green.

Sage stifled the laugh that bubbled up in her throat. "Nobody has figured me out, Mr. Lawson. Not my father, not my mother. Mama and

Papa let me go to medical college because they were afraid I would run away if they didn't. But they didn't understand.''

Now that her medical studies were concluded, the one thing she missed was being kept busy. Too busy to dwell on why she sometimes felt restless, as if her skin had shrunk overnight. She liked probing the mysteries of diphtheria and puerperal fever, liked finding out what was true and what was old wives' tales or just superstition.

But what was beneath her *own* surface was a mystery she didn't want to poke into.

''And just what have you figured out?'' The words leaped out of her mouth before she could catch them.

He twisted to face her again. ''You sure you want to know?''

''Of course. Though I doubt very much your observations will prove insightful.''

''Well, you're not gonna like this, but here goes.'' He looked straight into her eyes. ''You're all locked up inside. Afraid to feel things.''

''I most certainly am not! Whatever gave you such a ridiculous idea?''

He held her gaze without smiling. ''The fact that you swim with your eyes closed. Like you don't want to...I don't know, let yourself go and enjoy it, maybe.''

''That is presumptuous, Mr. Lawson.'' To give herself something to do, she flapped the reins, then realized every step the mare took brought her closer to him.

''You can call me Cord, Doc. You've seen me half-dressed, and I've seen you, well, vice versa. I think maybe we've been introduced good enough.''

''Mr. Lawson!''

He didn't even blink. ''You're right about the 'presumptuous' part, though.'' Again, he twisted to scan the trail ahead. ''I don't have a lot of fine manners to trip over,'' he called over his shoulder.

''You are certainly correct on that score,'' Sage murmured.

''So,'' he continued, ''I just say what I think. I'm not wrong very often.''

Sage took her time about answering. She drew in a long breath, expelled it, drew in another. ''You are wrong this time, Mr. Lawson.''

''Cord,'' he reminded her. ''You know, I've only seen you smile three times in two days, Doc. Once was when you swam the river. The point is, you were a little scared, but it felt good, didn't it?''

She swallowed instead of replying. Her father had taught her it was bad manners to argue on the trail, but she was so mad she felt like heaving the canteen at him. Tears stung her eyes. She straightened her shoulders.

"Well, Cord, I am not smiling now."

"You think about it, Doc. I know you're riding with me to do good for your fellow man. Might be this journey could do you some good, too." He moved forward at a faster pace and this time did not look back.

Sage reached behind the saddle and grabbed the first thing her fingertips encountered. Her camisole. She didn't alter her pace, didn't make a sound. But that old feeling of restless hunger was back, flooding her entire being until she wished she could just jump out of her skin and escape.

She used the garment to dab at her eyes until they reached a grassy clearing. When Cord called a halt, she wadded up the muslin and stuffed it under her saddle.

Chapter Six

The trail wound up through the timber, then reached a lush green meadow fed by a gurgling stream. The doctor kicked her horse into a canter and caught up with Cord.

He didn't want her any closer. He resisted an urge to dig in his spurs and gallop away from her, but he guessed she'd eaten enough of his dust for one day. The wind was picking up, so it was even worse now.

For the next quarter mile they rode side by side through the camas and meadow rue without saying a word. The quiet didn't seem to bother her, but it got under Cord's skin in a hurry. Not as much as those undergarments, fluttering from the back of her saddle in the warm afternoon wind, but enough that his already parched tongue felt like a dried corncob. He couldn't wait until it got dark and they made camp. He'd take a couple of pulls at the whiskey flask, roll himself up in his blanket and forget how raw and hungry his nerves felt. Another hour until sundown. He had to hold it together until then.

He glanced at the sky, then at the thick forest of maples and blue spruce covering the mountains ahead. The wind lashed the branches and the sighing sound set his teeth on edge.

Her voice at his side jolted him. "Tell me something, Mr. Lawson?"

"Depends what you want to know." He knew his reply sounded surly, but some instinct told him to duck and run, not answer questions. She was full of questions.

"I want to know who you were chasing. Before you needed a physician's services, I mean."

"I don't think you do."

Her eyes blazed like two purple amethysts. "Don't tell me what I want! I hate it when someone thinks for me."

"I still don't figure you want to know."

"But I'm interested! I've always been curious about things I don't know."

"That why you chose to be a doctor?"

"Well, yes, as a matter of fact. My baby brother died of diphtheria when I was ten. The day we buried him I decided I wanted to know why he died. I wanted to know what a doctor would have done to save him.''

Cord's gut tightened. ''Some things in life you can't control.''

''It is ignorance that leaves one vulnerable. At least that is what I fervently believe.''

He snapped his jaw shut and counted to ten. ''You're one of those goddamned 'truth will make you free' types, is that it? You think if you dig up enough facts, you can just take charge of the outcome. Choose hell or happiness. Life or death.''

''Of course, within reason. Things you know are the means to understanding life. It follows that if one understands, one can correct what is wrong. Illness, for instance.''

''Let me tell you something, Doc. Real life is mostly about feelings, not facts. Feeling hungry. Feeling tired. Feeling the sun on your back. Feeling good, or…feeling like you want to die.''

She sniffed. ''That is an extremely limited philosophy.''

''Maybe. In the long run, it's the only one that matters.''

''Oh?'' Her eyes bored into his like two blue bullets. The wind lifted her hat brim, and she jerked it down tight. ''And just what exactly makes you so sure of that?''

"Managing to stay alive for thirty-seven years."

"But…what have you *done* with those years?"

"Laughed some. Cried some. Mostly tried to enjoy them." He didn't think she really wanted to know about the black times.

"Is that *all?*"

"That's all. How old are you, Doc?"

"Um, well, I'm—" She drilled him with those eyes again. "That is a distinctly personal question, Mr. Lawson."

"Yeah. But I've seen you with half your duds off, so you want me to guess?"

"I will be twenty-six in December," she said quickly.

"And what have you done with *your* years?"

She straightened her spine just enough to make him smile. "I have used them to investigate. To understand about life. I have studied. Learned."

"Have you enjoyed yourself?" He wanted to add something about sensual pleasure, but one glance at her tightened mouth and he thought better of it.

"Reasonably, yes. I have a purpose in life. An honorable calling. I am…content."

He snorted. "Content! You don't understand jack squat about life, Doc."

"I do, too! I understand a great deal about living a worthwhile life. You are a footloose thirty-seven-year-old drifter who doesn't belong anywhere. It is *you* who doesn't understand about life."

He gritted his teeth. "You think so, do you?"

"I think so, yes. I *know* so."

"Well, you're dead wrong, Doc." She was a prissy, stuck-up female with a brain too big for her britches. He clenched his jaw even tighter. "And if the opportunity presents itself, I'll show you what I mean."

"You will do no such thing!"

"Not much you can do to stop me, is there? I always have enjoyed rubbing some know-it-all, overeducated pilgrim's nose in the messy part of life."

She rode on ahead with one hand clutching her hat, the purple feather bobbing and flopping as the wind picked up. With her other hand she vainly tried to poke escaping strands of dark hair under the crown.

Oh, the hell with it. Now was as good a time as any.

He caught up with her and grabbed the mare's bridle, pulling the animal to a halt beside him.

She pinned him with an icy look. "Just what do you think you're doing?"

"Teachin' you something," he growled. He swept the battered Stetson off her head and sent it sailing away on the breeze. Without pausing to think, he dug his fingers into her hair, raked out the pins that secured her neat bun and lifted the loosened strands away from her scalp. The wind ruffled the waves about her face.

"What *are* you doing?" She tried to back out of his grasp, but he tightened his grip.

"This." He combed his fingers through the dark, silky mass, let the breeze play with it. She swatted at his wrists.

"Stop that this instant!"

Instead, he tilted her head so the wind whipped through her flying hair. "You feel it?"

He scarcely heard her answer. *He* felt it—the wind on his face, her hair against his skin. Oh, boy, did he feel it. The sensations curled inside his chest, his belly and right on down to his toes.

"Feel it?" he rasped again. "It's a gift. Free for the taking, not like other things in life. All you have to do is open yourself up to it."

He released her, snatched at the buttons on his shirt and flung it away. His hat followed. He turned toward the wind, lifted his face to the rushing air and let it caress his cheeks and neck.

His arms lifted away from his sides, hands stretched out, fingers flexing. "Damn, that feels good!"

Sage stared at him, trying to corral unruly strands of her hair as the breeze slapped them against her face. His hands captured hers, pulled them to her sides. "Just sit still," he hissed. "Don't fight it."

Pinned, she sat as motionless as she could, facing into the warm air that licked and nuzzled her skin. Like hundreds of little cats' tongues, flicking her nerve endings into awareness.

What was happening to her? An hour ago she'd felt confident and in control. But he had changed that. Now she felt...well, she didn't know what she felt, exactly. Trembly. Excited in an odd way.

All at once something unlocked inside her and she wanted to cry.

He stepped his mount closer, dropped his hands to her shoulders. Desperately she tried to control the shuddering of her body. She would *not* weep. Only silly, overwrought females wept at every little thing. Hysterics, her professors termed them. Women who needed a man. Babies. *Oh, what was the matter with her?*

"Never cried for him, did you? Your baby brother."

"N-no. Mama did. She screamed and carried on, but I couldn't. I...I had to take care of Mama."

"You locked it all inside," Cord said.

The dam within her broke. She nodded, hiccuping with harsh gulping sounds as she choked back her sobs. "I don't want to do this," she gasped. "It hurts. It *hurts*."

"Do it anyway." He cupped one hand behind her head and pulled her forward, pressed her forehead hard against his neck.

He looked beyond her as she wept, felt his throat tighten. After a long minute, he closed his eyes.

Chapter Seven

Sage cried until Cord's neck and the upper part of his chest were wet with tears. His skin felt warm and sticky, but he didn't move. He held her while her shuddering lessened and the sobs subsided to an occasional hiccup. Over her head he watched puffy white clouds sail to the west, driven by the wind. Might be a storm blowing up.

He brought his mouth to her ear. "Can you ride?"

She nodded against his chin.

"There's a well-protected campsite ahead, about an hour as the crow flies."

"How far on horseback?" she murmured.

Cord hesitated. He didn't want to let her go. She felt good in his arms, soft and warm and alive. Zack Beeler had given him an orphaned baby bobcat on his ninth birthday; the animal had snuggled against his chest and Cord had laughed with joy. Later, when he had to turn the cat loose after it clawed him, he had wept.

"Another three hours. Switchbacks," he explained.

Her shoulders slumped. "That means 'up,' doesn't it?"

"Not too far. Just enough to give me a view of the valley." No need to tell her how crucial it was that he see an approaching horseman. His quarry would be a fool to follow them, but with a killer you never knew.

Cord had spent some hours trying to think like that son-of-a-dog Suarez. What would a desperate man do if you'd watched him shoot someone and then ridden away? Would he hightail it back to Chihuahua? Or come after Cord, to make sure he didn't tell anyone about it?

She lifted her head, pulled herself upright in the saddle and swiped her shirtsleeve under her reddened nose. It was such a little-kid gesture his heart turned over. God, he hated to see a hurt thing.

Without her hat, one cheek had sunburned; the other, the one that had been buried against his neck, looked dead white. She'd need spirits.

Cord licked his lips, hoping there was enough whiskey for both of them.

He dismounted to retrieve the shirt and hat he'd flung into the wind, then found her gray Stetson lodged in a huckleberry bush, the purple feather looking ragged but still bobbing upright. There was no sign of the hairpins.

He steadied her horse, laid the reins in her open palm. "Couldn't find any of your hair doo-dads. Can you make do with a piece of string?"

In answer she untied the red bandanna at her throat and rolled it into a soft rope. Lifting her arms, she slipped the fabric under the mass of dark waves and looked up at him. He wished she hadn't.

Without dropping her gaze, she looped the bandanna into a knot, catching the hair at her neck. Cord slapped his hat on his head and shrugged into his shirt, not bothering to button it. He'd let the warm air dry his tear-drenched skin.

And he'd try like hell to think of something other than the way her shirt pulled over her breasts. Latin verbs, maybe. Brands of cut to-bacco.

"Ready?" The word rasped out of a dry throat.

"Yes."

Her eyes looked puffy and red rimmed. Her hands clasped the reins with such a loose grip he wasn't sure she knew what she was doing.

"I am ready," she added. The words came out slow and flat.

Like hell she was. Part of him wished they could camp right here so she wouldn't have to drag herself any farther. The rest of him knew he couldn't take the risk. He'd push her for her own safety, and his.

Sometimes he hated the life he'd chosen. But he was already more than halfway across this particular river; if he turned back he'd have nothing. If he turned back, he'd drown.

He kneed his horse forward, and without a word she fell in behind. He'd have to hand it to her. Even worn out by her crying jag, she was still a fighter. There weren't many women like that—half-dead and still in the saddle. His mother had done that same thing the night he was born. He always thought that kind of grit had died with her.

The mare plodded steadily forward, right up to the hindquarters of the lead horse. Sage hadn't noticed that Cord had stopped, but even when she realized it, she made no move to dismount.

In a minute or two he'd move on, and she'd

have to dig her heels into her mount again. Her legs felt so lifeless she wondered if she could manage such a feat. Unable to lift her head, she studied the tiny tear in the hem of her riding skirt and waited.

Two large hands closed around her waist, tipped her sideways and pulled her off the horse. Then she was aware of being carried, her chin bumping against a pearl button, the smell of horse and sweat in her nostrils. He could toss her in the river for all she cared; her mind and her body were no longer communicating.

Instead of cold water, she felt a soft spongy mass of something under her buttocks. She reached out one hand and patted the material. Pine needles. Oh, thank the Lord. The pungent scent was the sweetest thing she'd ever smelled!

Sage leaned sideways until her shoulder hit the nest of pine boughs, then she pulled her knees up to her chest and closed her eyes. She heard footsteps, then the sound of a saddle being lifted and plopped on the ground near her. Two saddles.

Bless the man. She wouldn't have to ride anymore today.

More noises. Saddlebag straps opening, the clink of tin plates and a frying pan. Something gurgling out of a bottle. Then a voice, low-pitched and hoarse, but oddly gentle. ''Here, drink this.''

A hand guided her fingers to a tin cup. Water, she hoped. She sniffed at the contents.

Whiskey. It didn't matter a whit; it was liquid. She swished it around in her mouth to wash away the trail dust, and swallowed. She couldn't even feel it going down.

She laid her head back on the pine needles, set the cup in front of her. Whenever she garnered strength enough, she took a swig, tipping the cup sideways to her mouth. Between sips she watched Cord move around the camp, building a fire in a circle of already blackened stones. He'd been here before.

He dropped two bedrolls on the other side of the now crackling fire, and she listened to the horses crunching grass some yards away, nickering in contentment. Somewhere a stream burbled. She was filthy, and the thought of a bath tugged at her, but she had no will to stand up, let alone search in her possibles bag for a bar of soap.

The sun dipped below the trees, and the sky began to flare with a warm rose-gold glow. Cord disappeared for a few moments, then knelt beside the fire and balanced a bucket of water on the stones. Beside that he set the frying pan, and the next thing she knew bacon sizzled and an enamelware pot began to bubble.

Coffee! The man could read her mind. And he could cook. Well, maybe not biscuits, but right now she'd eat anything he set before her, even fried rattlesnake. She watched him set a flat rock on top of the bacon to keep it from curling up. It worked better than her mama's fancy bacon press.

Sage closed her eyes and let herself float. How absolutely delicious it felt to lie still and just listen to the sounds—the wind sighing through the treetops, a thrush warbling from a thicket of vine maple. The fire snapping like hot popcorn.

Cord moved about the camp with slow, deliberate steps. A spoon clunked. The bird ceased its song, then resumed. Sage felt warmth creep into her bones.

She ate most of a plate of smoke-flavored beans and bacon before she began to feel even half-alive. Nothing had ever tasted so good, not even her father's special fried trout. Something Cord sprinkled over her plate added a tang she couldn't identify.

"What is that sharp flavor?"

He glanced up from his heaping plate, fork poised midway to his mouth. "Mexican pepper.'' He chewed a mouthful, watching her reaction.

''It feels cool on my tongue, then hot in my throat.''

His eyes held hers. ''You like it?''

''I'm hungry enough to like practically anything,'' she admitted with a laugh. ''Even fried rattlesnake.''

''The sensation, I mean. The peppery bite, and then the heat. You have to wait a few seconds to get the full effect.''

Sage nodded and held the next bite in her mouth before swallowing. This time her lips burned.

''You're not much aware of feeling things, are you, Doc? You kinda button up tight and skirt around them.''

''My responses to life are my own concern.''

Cord chuckled at the frost in her voice. ''Yeah, that's true enough. Still, you say you like to investigate things, so how come you haven't done more exploring in regard to yourself?''

''Because,'' she said with a hint of steel in her voice, ''I already know about myself. I understand how my mind works. I know when I am ill or happy or sad or…'' she eyed a strip of crisp bacon ''…hungry.''

"That's all, huh?"

"Is that coffee I smell?" she said quickly.

He set his plate aside, got to his feet and filled her mug. Before he gave it to her, he splashed in a bit of whiskey and then took a sip. His dark eyebrows drew together briefly and an assessing look crossed his face while he held it in his mouth. Finally, he swallowed, nodded and handed the cup over.

For some reason the gesture made her feel good inside. Cared for. Not even her father would check how his camp coffee tasted.

"Getting back to how things feel," he continued. "How about this afternoon, back at the meadow?"

She gave him a blank look. "The meadow?"

"You remember. The wind came up and I—"

"Oh, yes. I do recall. You threw away my hat and…and then I started to cry."

"All you recall is crying? Not the breeze ruffling your hair or the smell of the wild buckwheat?"

"N-no. I must have missed something."

"Yep. You most definitely missed something, Doc. You spent near an hour sobbing like your heart was broken, and you didn't notice the things that might've helped ease the hurt. Life gives us plenty of hurt. It's those other things we need to help us stay sane.''

Sage stared at him. ''Are you prescribing for me? I would remind you that *I* am the physician.''

''You want to get educated?''

''Yes!'' She snapped out the word, and then another. ''No!''

''Make up your mind, Doc. You'll most likely have just this one chance, so take it or leave it.''

''Why will I have just one chance?''

''Because I'm the one who can teach you, and we've only got seven or so days left.''

Sage bit the inside of her cheek, considering. She was tempted—no, that was the wrong word. *Tempted* pertained to carnal matters. She was…curious. What could this man—a life-hardened rolling stone, a bounty hunter, for heaven's sake—possibly know that would be of value to her? Besides how to rip hairpins from a woman's chignon and make the most eye-watering coffee she'd ever tasted?

A lazy smile curved his lips. ''Scared?''

She sat up straighter. ''Certainly not.''

''You're lying,'' he said quietly.

''No, I am…'' Oh, yes she was, she admitted. Scared and lying both. The prospect of whatever he had in mind set something aquiver in her belly, as if she sensed that what she might learn would change her. She wanted it, whatever it was, and at the same time she wanted to shut herself off from it and flee.

He said nothing, just shoveled food into his mouth, studying her with those unnerving green eyes.

"Very well, I accept your offer."

Still he said nothing. When his plate was empty he set it on the ground, stood up and came toward her. "How are you feeling right this minute?"

"Tired. My head aches and my eyes feel hot."

"How about the rest?"

"The rest?"

"From your neck down. There's more to being alive than having a brain that works."

She hesitated. "Well, I am...filthy. And I feel sticky all over. My skin feels like sandpaper." She thought she saw the glimmer of a smile, but she couldn't be sure.

"I know just what you need." He turned toward the fire, lifted the steaming bucket of water off the rocks and strode toward her.

"Strip," he ordered.

Chapter Eight

Why the devil did I think this was a good idea? A bucket of warm water, a bar of soap, a washcloth—it all seemed straightforward. She'd wash off and feel better. Pretty simple.

Until she rose without questioning his order and began to unbutton her shirt.

Cord wanted to watch, but for some reason he couldn't. He turned away, heard her boots thunk onto the ground, imagined her skirt dropping at her feet. And she wore nothing underneath, he recalled. God almighty. He remembered the lacy white camisole and ruffled drawers pinned to the saddle blanket on the back of her mare. The garments were dry now, but what the hell.

To keep his mind on the business at hand, he began to talk. "This is real soothing, Doc. You can do it every time you feel dusty or hot or just plain low in spirits.''

''Mmm,'' she murmured. He knew she was standing there behind him without a stitch on. He ached to turn his head and take a peek. At the mere thought his trousers felt tighter.

He decided he needed to talk some more. ''Now, Doc, don't just scrub yourself off like you're a dirty plate. What's important is to feel every inch of your skin and pay some mind to it. Go slow and smooth, so it feels good.'' He swallowed.

''I know how to take a spit bath, Mr. Lawson.'' The oh-so-superior note in her voice made him want to yell at her. He swallowed again. Yelling at her would hurt her feelings.

''I'll just…clean up the skillet down at the creek,'' he blurted. He strode away, hearing the splash of water behind him.

Scouring the skillet with wet sand didn't take near long enough. He was too aroused to go back to camp just yet, so he shucked his jeans, waded into the deepest part of the stream and took a long, cold dip. He stayed in until the skin on his fingers puckered and goose bumps prickled his forearms. When he was good and chilled, he slogged to the bank, paced up and down, letting the air dry him off, and pulled his boots and trousers back on.

Moving quietly out of long habit, he drew near the camp and caught a glimpse of her through the trees. The sight halted him in his tracks. Lord God in heaven.

She was slim, perfectly formed with small, pointed breasts and a softly rounded bottom. Except where she was sunburned, her skin looked like sweet, fresh cream. She turned to wash behind one knee, and the dark triangle of hair between her thighs made his groin tighten all over again.

He'd seen women before, but not like this one. He couldn't make himself move. He knew he should close his eyes, shut out the vision she made standing in the firelight with her dark hair tumbling over her shoulders. But he couldn't stop looking.

After she dried herself and slipped on her undergarments, he purposely rustled some dry branches to make noise and stalked into camp brandishing the clean skillet. Quick as a cat, she rolled herself into a blanket and curled up by the fire.

"All finished?" he asked, his voice tight.

"Yes," she answered.

"Warm?"

"Yes, warm." Her voice was noticeably softer.

"Feel better?"

She didn't answer.

He tramped over and looked down at her. Sound asleep. He couldn't help smiling. Seemed his "lesson" had just plain worn her out.

Cord cleaned the supper utensils, poured out the cold coffee and filled the pot with fresh water for morning. He dumped the bucket of wash water on a parched-looking wild azalea bush, checked the horses, paced twice around the fire pit. While the flames burned down to glowing coals and the stars winked to life above him, he did everything he could to keep from thinking about her. Not just the satiny skin that looked so delicate, and her female curves, and those breasts he'd like to stroke, but *her*. Dr. Sage West.

She was a plum that didn't know what ripe meant. He'd sure as hell like to show her, but some inner voice told him to stay clear. He couldn't say why exactly, but the message was burning into his brain. *Touch her and you'll regret it the rest of your days.*

A tight feeling crawled into his chest, spreading until he could scarcely suck air into his lungs. He wet his lips, then went to check the horses again.

Sage heard him moving around the camp. Her lids refused to open and after a while she gave up trying and just listened. His low voice spoke bits of nonsense to the horses, and then his boots thumped back toward the fire and stopped close by.

An irresistible urge to reach out and pat one leather toe seized her, but her arm wouldn't budge. Poor old boots. They didn't get any special attention the way the horses did. The thought was so irrational she wondered if she'd had too much whiskey.

Beside her a blanket flapped, and the next thing she heard was measured breathing at her back. He'd bedded down next to her without even asking permission! He lay so close she could feel his exhalations on the nape of her neck.

In spite of herself, she smiled. Somehow she didn't mind. Didn't mind at all.

Cord waited until he couldn't stand it any longer, then he reached one arm across her midsection, carefully spread his fingers and pulled her back against his chest so her spine pressed his breastbone. She murmured something that sounded like "dress."

He didn't care what she said, just as long as she didn't move. He didn't want to think too much about what he was doing. He was like any other man—they all put their pants on one leg at a time, didn't they? He was having a perfectly normal male reaction to being this close to a female.

But she wasn't like any other female. Yeah, he wanted her, but he'd do nothing. He didn't have the right.

Sage nestled against his warm, solid body and sighed with pleasure. How good it felt to be near him. To touch him.

He had shown her something today she had never really thought about before. Pain was inevitable in life; suffering was optional. The key—for him, anyway—lay in offsetting the bad feelings with good feelings. Opening oneself to…well, pleasure. Smelling the roses along the way. *Eat, drink and be merry, for tomorrow we may not be here.*

She could never do that—live in such a hedonistic manner. She was here on God's earth to relieve others' suffering, not waste time enjoying what felt good at the moment.

She liked this man, Cord Lawson. Respected him, even.

But his way was not her way. He had no obligations to anyone other than himself, while she had a sworn duty to put other people, her patients, first.

She closed her eyes and tried to let her thoughts swirl away with her fatigue. She imagined the blood flowing in her body, the life-giving plasma pushed along in her arteries with every beat of her heart. The line between life and death was so fine; one minute a person breathed in and out, swallowed, cried. The next minute he didn't.

In her mind's eye she saw her baby brother lying gray and motionless in the cradle her father had made of woven willow boughs. Alive, and then suddenly not alive.

On impulse she rose up on one elbow and stared down at the man lying beside her, sound asleep. His breathing was slow and quiet, his heart pumping in regular rhythm under his shirt. She could see the blue cotton flutter with each beat.

She studied his closed eyelids, the black lashes against his tanned skin. Then she leaned down, tipped her head to bring her ear close to his chest and listened to the air pull in, out, in.

She stretched out her hand and laid her palm on the spot. Under her flesh his heart pulsed, again, again. Warmth from his body crept up her arm. Her fingers tingled with it.

He was alive…and foreign. Male to her female.

Did other women watch a man at night, when no one would know? Why did they? Why did she watch Cord—to make sure he was alive?

Of course he was alive. He was far too alive, like a hot coal dropped into her sterile, cool existence. Something that must be handled carefully.

Her gaze came to rest on his mouth. Closed in sleep, the well-formed lips looked firm. She wanted to touch him there, see if his lips were warm or cool, but she dared not. They were warm, she knew. Even though he was a stranger, aloof at times. Hard. Solitary. Everything about the man seemed warm to her.

It was such an odd contrast—the ice man with a heart of fire—that she almost laughed aloud. She touched her fingers to her own lips, felt the sigh of her breath on her fingertips. She, too, was warm. Alive.

The thought made her smile again. She was twenty-five years old, and just now waking up.

By midmorning Sage had recovered enough of her physical strength to keep up the pace Cord set through the thick forest and down the dry side of the mountain. As they moved steadily eastward, the trees began to thin out as the trail climbed once more to the timberline.

By noon, Cord had stopped only once to rest the horses. He pushed them hard.

But he pushed himself harder. Since sunup he had seemed preoccupied.

When he slowed at a sharp switchback, she called out. "How much farther?"

"Another couple of hours."

Sage eyed him. "By crow or horseback?"

"Straight ahead and steady." There was no hint of laughter in his voice. He was worried about something. The wounded man, perhaps?

"Who is with this injured person now?"

"An old Indian woman. A friend," he added at Sage's sudden intake of breath. "They call her Two Branches. She's a medicine woman."

"She will resent the intrusion of a white doctor."

"She's the one who sent me for a doctor," he said shortly. "Said 'big medicine' was needed for the white man's evil."

"Evil!"

"To the Paiute, a bow and arrow is an honorable weapon. A rifle is evil."

A chill swept over her, even though sweat trickled down her neck. "Cord?"

"Yeah?"

"What if it's too late? What if…"

He said nothing. He moved his mare into the lead position and Sage watched the sway of the animal's rump ahead of her. Frustration tightened her rib cage. How could he cut himself off from things like that? Just keep riding as if…as if it didn't matter?

"Cord! Cord, wait." She kicked her own mare hard and caught up with him. His dark hat was tipped low against the sun.

"Cord?"

When he turned toward her, she wished she hadn't spoken. Tears shone in his eyes.

Stunned into silence, she reined up.

He didn't say a word, just pulled his horse to a stop and sat there looking straight ahead. After a long while he looped the reins around the pommel, dismounted with the slow, easy motion she'd grown used to, and came toward her.

She dismounted as well, and moved to meet him. "What is it?"

He said nothing, just kept coming. When he reached her he stepped in close and folded his arms around her. "Don't move," he said in a quiet voice. "And don't talk. Just…be here."

"Cord, it is highly unusual to embrace one's doctor on the trail like this."

"Yeah," he said with a low sigh. His arms tightened around her and she heard him swallow.

"Yeah," he said again. "I know."

She waited, sensing instinctively he would speak when he wished to and not before. For some reason he needed her at this moment.

"You reminded me of something I didn't want to think about," he said at last.

She nodded against his hard, warm shoulder. "Something that hurts," she said. "The pain is in your eyes."

He set her away from him far enough to look into her face. His eyes were wet. "I need you," he said. "Don't ask questions, just let me…"

"Let you what?"

"Hold on to something, Doc."

"Is this another one of your 'feel-good lessons'?" She spoke the words gently, hoping to ease the tension she heard in his voice.

"God, yes," hc breathed. "Only this time you have to come with me." He pulled her forward, rested his lips against her forehead. "Sage."

She looked up, into his eyes, and with a low murmur he covered her mouth with his.

Chapter Nine

She'd been wrong. At the first touch of his lips moving over hers, asking and then taking, Sage knew she had missed something in life. Something so simple, so elemental she marveled how she could have lived twenty-five years without discovering it. And now that she knew, how could she live beyond this glorious moment without having it again? And again.

Cord's mouth was warm and dry, his tongue hot and so commanding her belly curled into a shaky knot of desire. With each passing second the sensations spiraled—the feel of his mouth, the taste of him, the heat. The scalding search for more. Deeper. Slower.

No man had ever touched her like this, taken her body and her soul and given them back to her suffused with a sense of belonging. A heady, uninhibited joy built inside her until she wanted to weep.

He broke free, groaned and kissed her again. Her breasts, even her most intimate place, swelled, aching with hunger.

At last Cord set her away from him and tried to control his ragged breathing. She swayed on her feet, her eyes still closed, a faint smile curving her mouth. The look on her upturned face made his insides turn over.

"This is only a horseback guess, but I'd say you enjoyed that."

She ran the pink tip of her tongue over her lips. "I am indebted to you, Mr.—Cord."

His breath hitched. "Indebted? You're the first woman who's ever said that after I kissed her. Indebted for what?"

She tipped to one side and he tightened his fingers on her shoulders, steadying her.

"For things you cannot possibly imagine."

Oh, he could imagine, all right. He felt a booted foot kick him hard in the gut. She wanted him. He'd shown her something about herself she hadn't known before—that she could feel passion. And it had knocked her plumb off balance.

But he had no right. She wasn't a cheap bit of calico. Right this minute, though, he'd give anything if she were. *Lord God, deliver me from Good Women!*

When she spoke again, her words made sense, but her voice sounded soft and unfocused, as if she was dreaming. "Perhaps we should mount and ride?"

Mount and ride? She had no idea what those words conjured in his imagination. His erection swelled. He stepped away so she wouldn't feel it, then wished he hadn't. He wanted her to feel it—feel him. Wanted to push close to her, so close she would...

"Yeah, we'd best keep moving." He took a deep breath and cleared the hoarseness from his throat. "Cabin's about an hour ahead."

"Cabin?"

He turned her toward her mare, placed the reins in her fingers. He could boost her up, but he didn't dare lay his hand on that rounded, inviting behind.

"A miner's shack. Somebody built it and abandoned it. I use it as a place to hole up when...sometimes."

"When what?" She mounted without effort, swinging a long, skirt-swathed leg up and over the horse's rump. Cord tried not to watch.

"When I'm cold. Worn-out." *When I'm so lonesome I start talking to rocks and pine trees.*

"Does anyone else ever go there?"

He clenched his jaw tight. The question caught him off guard, and for a moment his chest felt like somebody had stomped all over it with spurred boots. "Not usually."

"But my patient with the gunshot wound is there now, waiting for us, is that correct?"

Cord pulled himself into the saddle and met her clear-eyed gaze. "That's correct."

"Then I shall compose my mind about what has happened between us and tend to business. Get up there, Ginger."

He fell in beside her, near enough to detect the faint scent of pine on her skin but not so close he'd be tempted to reach out and touch her.

No good. He moved ahead. It was safer not to look at her, either. Damn, he'd never ached so bad for a woman before. Why should *she* affect him so strongly? There were other women. For him there would always be women. They made him feel good, whole and worth something more than just a smart tracker with a quick gun hand. In return, he made them happy, or so they said.

There wasn't a female on this earth he couldn't replace or ride away from.

Except for this one. He liked her. Liked her quickness and her wit. He liked her body, too, but the connection he felt had more to do with minds than bodies.

Was that why kissing her had left him feeling like he'd been run over by a stampeding herd? Because it was *her*—Sage—clinging to him, opening to him, not some nameless piece of skirt who didn't matter?

Sage mattered. The question was why?

They reached a lazy stream, only ankle deep, and with each splash of the horses' hooves the puzzle circled about in his head. Why? Why? *Why?*

Suddenly Cord straightened. Hell's bells. *You damn fool. You've got the lady doctor stuck so deep in your craw you can't think clearly.*

That was dangerous in itself. With a double-talking murderer like Suarez somewhere out there, it was suicidal. Especially after what had happened the first time Cord had found him.

Them.

Despite the hot sun on his back, a prickle of gooseflesh peppered his forearms. Best not dwell on it now. Just get to the cabin and take it one step at a time.

"Tonight," Sage said with conviction in her voice.

Cord shot her a look over his shoulder. "How's that?"

"I...I was thinking out loud."

"About tonight?"

"And other matters. My patient, for one."

He looked back again. "What about tonight?"

She hesitated, wetting her lips. "I was wondering what I was going to do."

"You mean where you're going to sleep?"

"No. That is, not exactly. More like *whether* I am going to sleep."

He fell back to keep pace beside her. "You slept fine last night. Like a cat full of cream."

"I had less to occupy my mind last night."

Cord swallowed. "You want some advice, Doc? Don't think so much."

"That is easy for you to say. For you, nothing is at risk."

It surprised him that she was so direct. Most women would pussyfoot around what she was facing.

"Think so, do you?"

"Yes," she said quietly. "I think so."

The fragrance of pine and dry grass hung on the breeze, and Sage's heart lifted. The air smelled sweet and sharp and clean, and she enjoyed breathing it in. She was beginning to notice things, small things. Pleasant scents. The pretty sound of creek water burbling over stones, or the *twing-towit* of a meadow bird. Things that felt good—the warm sun on the backs of her elbows, the puff of cool wind against her cheek. Cord's mouth on hers. His hands…

She had entirely too much to think about! This wasn't as simple and uncomplicated as a textbook on anatomy or diseases of the liver, which she could read and understand in a matter of hours. Her head was full of him and the unexpected things he made her feel.

Questions nagged at her. Had he kissed many women? Perhaps even taken them to bed?

Had they been soft and pretty and willing, or had he molded them to his desire with touches and kisses like the ones he had given her?

Oh, what did it matter if there were others? Her concern was about herself, why she stood here so close to him she could smell the faint odor of coffee on his breath, wanting him to touch her again.

Lord knew, she would not sleep one single minute tonight.

The trail wound on ahead of them, meandering through a stand of shiny-needled firs, around a copse of salal and vine maple, and then it suddenly petered out. Cord kept moving forward at the same steady pace. Obviously he knew exactly where he was, knew every inch of the ground over which he rode.

Sharp-edged fear cut into Sage's belly. If he moved out of her sight, she would be hopelessly lost. She kicked Ginger's flanks and trotted forward until she rode beside him.

The cabin appeared out of thin air. One moment she was guiding her mount around a vine-covered fallen log, the next she spied a structure that blended into the landscape so perfectly it was nearly invisible. A stone's toss from the timberline, the weathered structure of rough-hewn wood nestled within the last thinning stand of fir and jack pine. Beyond it, the bare mountain rose, melting into a sky washed with rose and peach as the sun sank.

Sage slowed her laboring mare. What a god-forsaken place. She watched Cord approach the shack and tie his horse to a graying porch post, then stride through the plank door and disappear inside.

By the time she had dismounted and retrieved her black leather medical bag from behind the saddle, Cord stood in the doorway, waiting.

"Still alive?" she intoned as she climbed the porch step.

He took her elbow. "Barely. The Indian

woman, Two Branches, left water and some pemmican, but..."

Sage nodded. "He's too weak to eat."

An empty place yawned in her stomach. She calculated that six days had passed while the patient waited for Cord to return with help. Six days with a gunshot wound. She prayed it had not festered.

"Where is...?"

"In here." He pushed aside a makeshift curtain of four mismatched flour sacks stitched together. Sage drew in a breath and tried to calm her thudding heartbeat.

Late-afternoon sunlight dappled the narrow bed under the single window. A worn patchwork quilt mounded over a motionless figure beneath it. Her patient, she surmised.

The silence was not a good sign.

Cord moved forward and knelt by the head of the bed. "I've brought the doctor," he murmured.

No response. Cord's gaze met hers in a long look, but as she lifted the quilt he glanced away.

No. Oh, no.

The figure was breathing. That was the first thing that registered. The second was the sound—a faint, dry rattle punctuated by long pauses.

The third thing was what she least expected.

A mass of dark hair tumbled against the pillow.

Good Lord in heaven, a woman!

And one who was near death.

Chapter Ten

Sage bent over the still form on the bed, peeled the folded cloth away from the woman's upper back. A poultice of green moss was bound in place with a leather thong. Drawing her scissors from her bag, Sage slit the tie and let the moss fall into her hand.

The wound had sealed over, but the area around it was dark and swollen, the skin stretched to bursting over the angry-looking black knob in the center. Infected. It would take a miracle to save her.

The figure stirred. "Cord?" a weak voice said.

"Right here, Nita. Rest easy now."

Nita. So Cord knew the woman. A girl, really. She couldn't be more than seventeen. Sage watched the way his hand moved over the girl's forehead, grazed her cheek.

A hiccup of unexpected fury slammed into her chest, followed by a gasp of recognition. She was *jealous!*

She had no right to such feelings. She was here for one purpose only—to help. Not to wonder over the wave of possessiveness that swept through her. She'd come to heal, not to judge. Not to think.

The patient's eyelids fluttered open and the girl tried to smile. *"Buenos tardes, señora."*

Sage leaned close. "My name is Sage West, *señorita.* I am a doctor. *Doctora."*

The girl inclined her head toward Cord. *"Mi esposo."*

Very slowly, Sage straightened. *Husband?* Cord was her husband? The possessiveness dissolved into a hollow ache. *Cord was not free.*

She met his steady gaze across the expanse of quilt, read his feelings as plain as if they were words printed in a book. Anguish. Desperation. Hope. *Save her life,* his eyes pleaded, while the silence hummed around them. *I can explain.*

Whatever the situation, she could not think about it now. She slipped the scissors back into her medical bag, noticing how her hands shook.

Cord was a married man? She felt as if she'd been slapped hard by a cold, wet hand.

Worse, she was frightened. She had never treated such an awful wound. The girl had very little chance of surviving, but still Sage had to try. Now that she knew the girl's significance to Cord, she must do better than try; she must succeed. *I am a physician first, a woman second.*

"Get some water," she ordered. "And build a fire."

They worked side by side the rest of that day and all that night. Sage lanced the swollen head of the infection, but there was little drainage from the site. The poison had spread inward, gone deep into the girl's slight body. Deep inside she knew it was too late, but she could not give up.

She laid the steaming compress Cord handed her on the wound, watched him walk away to drop another towel in the pot of water boiling on the stove. His steps were unsteady, his face wooden.

Sage couldn't bear to look at him. *It is out of my hands, Lord. Don't let her die. Please.*

Nita lapsed into a drowsy stupor, rousing to awareness only when Sage changed the dressings on her back. "*Mamacita,*" she muttered at one point. "Tell Papa…tell Papa…"

Sage bent low. "Tell your papa what?"

"Antonio…"

Cord sucked in a breath.

"Antonio, he is my…" The girl drifted again into unconsciousness.

Sage looked up at Cord, standing by the bedside. "Who is Antonio?"

"Her… The man I'm chasing. Antonio Suarez. He's wanted for murder."

Sage nodded and bent to check the girl's heartbeat. Irregular. And so faint she could scarcely hear it. She needed to tell him.

"Cord." She swallowed hard before she could go on. "I cannot save her. It's gone too far."

"I know," he said, his voice dull. "I've seen gangrene before."

"It's gone too deep for surgery. Cutting it out would kill her."

"Yeah."

"I am sorry. So terribly sorry."

"How long?" he asked in a quiet tone.

Sage studied Nita's pale, sweat-sheened skin, watched her pull sporadic, uneven breaths through lips that had lost their color. "Before morning."

Cord said nothing. He took the dressing she handed him, walked to the stove and dropped it in the simmering water. He fished out another with a crudely carved wooden spoon, wrung it out when he could touch it, and reappeared at the bedside.

"She is beyond that now," Sage said gently. "Beyond anything we can do."

"Laudanum?"

She shook her head. "I think she is beyond that, too."

Cord bent and laid the hot cloth on Nita's exposed back. "I've got to do something for her, even if she doesn't need it now."

"Yes," Sage breathed. "I feel the same." She smoothed her palm slowly up and down Nita's bare arm. At least the girl might feel her touch, know she was being tended. Know she would not die alone.

"Can she hear?"

"Yes. It is the last sense to go."

Cord knelt at the head of the bed, brought his mouth close to the girl's ear. "Nita? Nita, you know that I..."

Sage scrambled to her feet. She couldn't bear to listen.

An hour later, Cord joined her where she paced on the porch. In the faint moonlight his face looked drawn and shadowed. He said nothing, just stood staring out into the night.

Her heart wrenched at his pain. She remembered all too well the agony she'd felt when her baby brother died. There were no words, just a heavy, suffocating blackness.

Back at the girl's bedside, Sage heard a murmur and bent close.

"Doctora," the thready voice uttered. "Hear me."

"I hear you, Nita. What is it?"

"Cord…"

Sage's pulse jumped. "Yes, your husband. *Esposo.* Shall I fetch him?"

"No. Listen…I must tell…"

"I am listening," Sage assured her.

"Papa hurt me. Cord take me away." She labored for a breath. "To be safe, he take me."

"Yes," Sage said. "I understand."

"No, *señora,* you do not. He marry me to keep safe. But…"

Sage's heart seemed to drop, cold and frozen, into her stomach. "But?" She lifted the girl's limp hand and held it in both of hers.

"No hemos hecho el amor. Never."

No hemos hecho? What was *hemos hecho?* "You mean you and Cord—?"

"Only with Antonio. Is sin. Big..." her eyelids fluttered shut "...big sin."

"God will forgive you, I am sure," Sage said, her voice choked.

"*Dios, sí...* He forgive. But not Cord. *Bueno hombre, mi espos—*"

Sage waited for her to finish the word, take another breath, but she did not. Oh Lord God, she was dead. She had been unable to save her.

Pain knifed into her belly, cut up through her chest to the backs of her eyes. This poor, troubled girl, grappling with her imagined sin, was at peace now. Sage smoothed one hand over the hot, damp forehead, gently closed the eyelids and knelt by the bed.

Help him, God. Help me.

At last she settled Nita's lifeless hand beside her on the quilt and went to get Cord.

Together they washed Nita's body, wrapped it in the quilt without speaking. When the sun rose, Cord took a shovel, walked away from the cabin and started to dig. Sage watched him, dazed with anguish, her mind unable to make sense of what had happened.

They buried Nita in the shelter of a windtwisted cypress, and piled rocks over the mound. Neither of them spoke a word until the last stone

was added, and then Cord stood at the head of
the grave, his hands clenched in front of him.

"Take care of her, Lord. She's been through
enough."

Chapter Eleven

Cord slid the spade into the opening beneath the front porch, then slowly straightened and turned toward Sage. "Saddle up."

"Now? Before…before breakfast? Before… Cord, we haven't slept since night before last. Don't you think we should—"

"Nope."

"But I am dead tired. And you are, as well. And hungry."

He moved toward her, his mouth a grim line. When he was so close she could see the hard glint in his eyes, he stopped.

"Look, Sage. I can't stomach staying here one more minute. You want to sleep in Nita's bed? Rattle around the cabin where she died?"

"Well, no. But we could camp outside the—"

"You could. I can't. There's too much of her here."

Sage stared at him in dawning awareness. "Why, you cared about her, didn't you? *Really* cared."

"Yes. What made you believe I didn't? But not like you're thinking. She was just a kid, but we traveled a lot of miles together. I'd guess you'd say we were…friends."

Some instinct warned her to skip the topic of his marriage. After Nita's confession about Antonio Suarez, who was apparently her paramour, Sage guessed their married state would be a sore point for Cord.

She could understand his reticence about staying up here where Nita had died; no doubt he felt a combination of sadness and guilt. She, too, felt a dreadful weight pressing down on her spirit. She had lost her very first patient. What kind of doctor was she if she couldn't save a life? The failure stung her like a red-hot poker.

In the next instant she made up her mind. "Yes, let's ride away from here. I feel sick all over at what has happened. So sick…"

Cord reached out and gave her shoulder a squeeze. "Yeah, me, too. And now there's—" He bit off the rest of the sentence and turned away.

She watched him saddle the horses and lead them forward. He tramped inside and returned with her medical bag, tied it on the mare's back and held the bridle, waiting for her.

Her head pounded. She couldn't seem to make her feet move, just stood there as if made of stone. Even her mind worked slowly. *Now there's what?*

This…whatever it was between Cord and her?

"Mount," he ordered in an even tone. He handed her the reins and stepped back. Once seated, she fought a rush of despair that washed over her, threatened to choke her. She wanted to vomit. Or scream. Or weep. Maybe all three.

She clamped her jaws together. *Oh, God, she'd wanted to save the girl. Just as she'd wanted to pluck her brother from the clutches of diphtheria.*

Why, God? Why?

Cord ran a swift glance over the shack, then motioned for her to move ahead of him.

"What about the cabin?"

"What about it?" he said.

"Are you just going to leave it like that? Isn't there anything you want from inside?"

"I'll be back someday. In the meantime, Two Branches can use it. She'll welcome the shelter come winter."

''Doesn't she live with her people?''

''Not anymore. She married an enemy warrior. He died in battle, but she couldn't ever go back. Women do the damnedest things.''

Again he scanned the vicinity, his gaze lingering on the fresh grave beneath the cypress, then turned his mount and spurred it forward. Without a word, Sage kicked her own mare and started after him, the rising sun at her back.

Dizzy with fatigue, concentrating hard on staying in the saddle, she jolted down the mountainside, too tired to think or even feel much. She knew from the dew still on the sparse clumps of grass that the early morning was chilly, but she didn't feel it. Her legs, her chest, her head felt numb, as if stuffed with cotton like a rag doll.

When they reached the timberline, Cord took the lead, heading straight into the thickest part of the forest. It was almost noon. Sage was so light-headed with hunger and lack of sleep, plus a mind-dulling grief, that she didn't hear Cord's order to stop, but plodded on until she felt a tug on her bridle.

''We'll stop here and rest.''

Oh, thank the Lord. ''And eat? Can we build a fire, fry some—''

''No fire,'' he snapped.

''But why?''

He gave her a long look and suddenly she knew. Her brain could not form complete thoughts, but she could grasp that much.

Someone was following them.

Cord jerked out of a sound sleep and lay motionless out of long habit. It was almost sundown, he noted. The sky overhead flamed with gold and then peach as he took stock of the situation.

The overgrown thicket of salal and vine maple surrounded them on three sides; he lay facing the only entrance, his loaded revolver under the saddle pillowing his aching head. If anyone rode in, he would be seen before he got close enough to fire.

But was it enough?

A sparrow hidden among the broad, yellow-green maple leaves started a trilling song, broke off, started again. A good sign. Birds usually shut up when something disturbed them or something foreign entered their vicinity. As long as they kept singing, Cord knew they were safe.

For the moment. He flicked his gaze from the spreading tree to Sage's still form, curled up a few feet away on her saddle blanket.

She wasn't asleep. Her violet-blue eyes were wide open, looking at him.

"Good morning," she said. She glanced at the now-rosy sky. "Or rather good evening. How long have we slept?"

Cord unkinked his back muscles and sat up. "Not long enough."

"What do we do now?"

"Move on down the mountain."

She rolled over onto one elbow. "At night?"

"There'll be a moon. There was last night, remember?"

Her expression changed. "I remember."

He started to speak, thought better of it, then changed his mind again. "I feel bad about this, Sage."

"Of course you do. You've lost your...wife. I feel dreadful, too."

He gave her an incomprehensible look, one she couldn't begin to decipher. Resignation? Determination? No, it was a strange mix of the two.

He stood up, hoisted the saddle onto one shoulder. "You ready?"

"Ready for what?" She eyed the revolver lying in the depression where his saddle had rested. "What is it you're not telling me, Cord?"

He turned toward the gooseberry thicket

where he'd picketed the horses. "Nothing much," he said after a slight hesitation. "Just that I'm sorry I got you into this mess. Guess I was so set on fetching a doctor for Nita I didn't think things through."

"Don't blame yourself, Cord. I don't. You couldn't have known how things would turn out. If anything, I am at fault for not being able to save her."

"It's more complicated than that."

"Complicated? In what way?"

Cord didn't answer. He couldn't think how to tell her. Maybe best leave it alone for the time being. He moved toward his mare, taking deliberate, quiet steps. "Just keep singing," he muttered to the burbling sparrow.

Sage was beside him in an instant, her saddle blanket folded in her arms. Strands of silky dark hair straggled free of the loose knot at her neck. He remembered she hadn't combed it in two days.

"Complicated how?" she repeated.

Cord made a small sound of annoyance. "You never give up, do you? You just keep worrying away at a crack until it splits open and you can see everything inside."

Sage tossed the blanket on the mare's back, stepped back and propped her fists on her hips.

"I am far too tired to worry at a crack, or anything else. As a matter of fact I am too tired to even listen to any more of your don't-upset-the-lady speeches. If you won't be honest with me, don't talk to me at all!"

Cord dropped his saddle where he stood. "Keep your voice down, dammit. And trust me."

"*Trust you!* Trust you?" she repeated in a lower tone. "You lied to me from the beginning."

"I have never lied to you. Or to anyone else."

"Then tell me what's wrong. No one in their right mind rides down a mountainside at night, unless they have to. I'm not so flummoxed by what has happened that I—"

"Just shut up, will you?" He grasped her shoulders and gave her a quick, hard shake. "Shut the hell up."

At that instant the sparrow broke off its song and Cord looked up, over her head. "Mount your horse," he ordered in a quiet voice. "We'll ride until sunup. I'll tell you when to stop, and then I'll explain some things."

When the rain started, a cold, drizzly mist that dampened and then soaked her sheepskin jacket and riding skirt, Sage considered doing the unthinkable: stopping the mare in her tracks, sliding off the animal's back and crawling into a thimbleberry thicket to sleep. She couldn't keep going, she just couldn't. Every muscle and bone in her body screamed for rest, and her mind—well, her thoughts weren't making much sense.

Hallucinations, that's what they were. She imagined the young Mexican girl, Nita, rising from her bed healthy and smiling. Next Sage conjured a crackling hot campfire, toasting her icy feet near the flames. Cord striding toward her, folding her into his arms.

If only she had been able to save the girl her heart would not feel like a dead tree stump, heavy and misshapen. She would not be stumbling down this pitch-black mountain with rain dripping off her hat brim. *If only.*

"What are you stopping for?" Cord's gravelly voice drifted to her through the fog of disjointed thoughts.

"I'm…I can't see the trail."

"Trust the horse. Just a few more hours and we can rest."

Sage willed her heels to nudge the mare's flanks, but try as she might, she could not move her legs. Her limbs were no longer connected to her brain.

"I can't, Cord. I just can't."

She heard his horse step toward her and stop. She tried to raise her head. "I can't," she repeated. "I am sorry."

His hand reached for the mare's halter. "I'll tie on a lead rope. Just stay in the saddle, that's all you have to do."

She nodded. Water sluiced off the front of her hat onto her thigh.

He unsnapped his saddlebag and she felt him fuss at the horse's head. After a moment he looped the reins about her clasped hands, pressed her thumbs down on top of the leather lines. "I know you're tired. Don't think about anything but holding on. Think about the hot coffee I'll brew when we stop."

"Hot coffee," she mumbled. "Will you build a fire?"

"Sure, we'll have a fire. And some whiskey. I think we both need it."

"I feel so sick about your...about Nita." Her voice seemed to come from somewhere outside herself.

"Yeah. Me, too." In a constricted voice he added, "Maybe if I'd—" He broke off. "Never mind. Let's just ride."

She nodded again, and when the horse stepped forward she commanded her stiff fingers to grip the reins.

Cord felt the tug of the lead rope he'd tied to his saddle, but even though he knew rationally that Sage was still seated on the horse behind him, he twisted to check. Yeah, still there. He just didn't know for how long. Her head drooped forward, her chin brushing her chest. A more thoroughly defeated-looking figure he'd never seen. Worse than some outlaws he'd brought in.

Goddamn, he felt sorry for her. Not because she was bone-tired and damp and her toes were probably freezing in those wet boots, but because he could see how much Nita's death had affected her. Probably shook her confidence in herself as a doctor right down to her britches.

Part of him wished he'd brought anyone but her up the mountain. What had he been thinking? She was a green doctor, and not only that, she was a woman.

Another, larger part of him was glad he'd found her. Just starting out on her medical practice as she was, she was bound to lose a patient sooner or later; in a funny way he wanted to be the one with her when it happened. She took the loss hard, and something inside him wanted to ease the pain.

At the same time, he was gut-wrenchingly sad about Nita. He'd been responsible for her for four years, since she was just a kid riding hell-for-leather out of Morelia after her father had beaten her. Cord had felt responsible for her ever since.

He felt responsible for her death. He'd liked her well enough, and she'd died because he'd been so hell-bent on getting that bastard Suarez. Cord hadn't known then about Suarez and Nita. That they were lovers.

It was all twisted up inside him. The bounty money for turning the murderer over to the authorities had kept food in Nita's pantry and store-bought dresses in her closet. Maybe Cord would feel better if she hadn't tried to run off with the outlaw. Maybe things would have turned out differently if Cord had given her a real marriage. If he'd loved her. Slept with her. Given her children.

Or maybe in the three days it took to get back to the cabin, he'd fallen half in love with someone else.

Okay, more than half.

His heart ached for Nita and for Sage. *What kind of a man did that make him?*

He didn't feel very good about any of it, he admitted. He hadn't had the right to touch Sage when they'd started up into the wilderness. He thought about that as his horse slogged on down the muddy trail toward civilization.

Now the problem was that thinking about Sage—about touching her again, holding her—was the only thing that kept him going. That and Antonio Suarez.

Chapter Twelve

By the time they reached the secret place on the east side of the mountain wilderness that Cord sometimes used for a camp, he was about done in. His mind craved respite from the thoughts that haunted him; his body craved sleep. A glance back at Sage told him she was at the end of her strength as well, hanging on by sheer willpower. He reined in his exhausted mare.

He liked this camp. It was well-hidden, sheltered in a grotto of overgrown deer fern within a thick stand of hemlock and pine. The rain had stopped, and the predawn air smelled so sharp and green it made his eyes water.

The effort required to lift his leg to dismount surprised him; his muscles were cold and tired.

Maybe he was getting old. He ached in places he'd never been aware of before.

Sage sagged over the pommel of her saddle, both hands still gripping the reins. Gently he pried her fingers away from the leather, then tugged her sideways so she toppled off the horse into his arms. Even fully clothed, she weighed no more than a sack of cornmeal.

She curled against his chest, tucked her head under his chin and made a mumbled noise. By damn, she was sound asleep.

He held her without moving, listening to her breathing, aware of the faint thump of her heartbeat through the damp jacket. Stepping carefully so she wouldn't wake up, he managed to tie both horses to an alder sapling using one hand, then walked into the small clearing he'd hacked out three summers ago. With the toe of one boot, he rolled the scattered kettle-size rocks into a rough firepit circle.

When he'd kicked together enough twigs and small branches to start a fire, he thought about putting her down.

But he didn't. He liked having her in his arms. Liked it so much he tramped three times around the camp perimeter with no particular chore in mind, just holding the soft, warm burden against his chest. Finally he snagged the blanket he'd tied under his rain poncho behind his saddle, flapped it open as best he could, and spread it close to the fire. Kneeling, he settled the sleeping form in his arms on top of the warm, dry wool. She didn't even whimper, just rolled into a tight ball.

The kindling blazed and snapped. He dumped on dry pinecones and chunks of wood he kept stashed inside a burned-out stump, then unsaddled the horses and fed them oats he'd kept dry in his saddlebag. He should get out of his wet clothes and eat something, but he wasn't hungry.

Not for food, anyway.

He retrieved another blanket, shucked off his boots and the rest of his clothes and turned his backside to the fire. Nothing better in the world than heat on an expanse of chilled skin. Might be what Sage needed, too.

"Doc?"

There was no sound but the hissing of the fire.

"Sage, wake up. You've got to take off your—"

She groaned and wriggled her body into an even tighter lump.

He spread the rain poncho near the fire, gathered the four corners of the blanket she lay on and lifted the entire bundle closer to the warmth. Then he knelt beside her.

"Sage? Sage, wake up." He waited, then removed her boots. Her socks were still dry, so he left them on, but he pulled off her jacket and unsnapped her damp riding skirt.

Still she slept. She'd get chilled if she lay all night like this. Should he stop? Go ahead and undress her?

To hell with propriety. He slid the denim skirt over her hips and down her legs, then started undoing her shirt fastenings. Half-asleep, she tried to help, but her fingers couldn't work the buttons through the holes.

Her undergarments were cold, but not wet. He wanted to remove them, too, but knew he didn't dare. It was risky enough to strip off her wet things and warm her up with his own body heat.

He draped their damp garments on an alder sapling to dry, propped both pairs of boots by the fire. She didn't even twitch.

Thank God Suarez was on the other side of the mountain. Cord couldn't keep his eyes open one more minute.

Without another thought of the outlaw or Nita or the whole damn mixed-up state of his heart, he stretched out beside Sage, folded the warm blanket over their bodies and pulled her close.

Some change in her breathing brought Cord out of a sound sleep to find her blue-violet eyes open and looking steadily into his. They faced each other, close but not touching. His arm rested over the mound of her hip. He should move away, but he didn't. He just plain didn't want to.

A shaft of sunlight touched her hair, highlighting the tangled dark strands with auburn. He said the first thing that came into his mind. ''You've got red hair.'' The observation was so irrelevant he groaned aloud.

''My grandmother had red hair.''

Cord wanted to tell Sage how beautiful her hair was, but something stopped him. Instead, he swallowed and said, ''The sun is up.''

Her slow, steady breathing sent intermittent warm puffs into his face. If he opened his mouth, he could almost swallow her exhaled air.

''How do you feel?'' His question hovered in the quiet, sun-warmed morning air like a butterfly uncertain where to land. Tension coiled in his chest as he waited for her response.

''I feel miserable.''

''It wasn't your fault,'' he said in a quiet voice.

''I feel responsible. I feel awful, just sick that I couldn't have done more. How arrogant of me, to think that I could save a life. Death is much stronger than I am."

"Only if you let it be. That is where the real battle is—inside us."

She stared at him.

"I feel lousy, too," he added. "She tried to shield him. Suarez, I mean. Nita caught the bullet he meant for me."

"What do *you* do, then, when you've failed and you feel miserable?"

Cord hesitated. "I...look for ways to feel better. Any way I can."

She didn't blink. "What ways?" Her eyes begged him for help.

"Whiskey sometimes. Doing things that feel good."

"What things?"

"The things I've been showing you—feeling the wind in your hair, swimming in the rain, smelling the grass. Listening to a meadowlark some mornings makes me glad I'm alive. Lying close to a warm fire, like we are now. And..." He decided not to finish that particular thought.

"And?" she prompted. "Tell me the rest, Cord. Please. And what?"

He thought about evading the question, or just plain lying. But she was asking how to live in the world where, God knew, things could be ugly. Where people died no matter how hard you worked to save them. Where hearts and bodies got pretty well beat up along the way.

He wouldn't lie to her.

"And...being with a woman."

He caught a flicker of something in her eyes. Interest? Disapproval? He couldn't tell. It was soul-jarring enough to think that he was baring his most private thoughts to her.

"Being with a woman," she murmured. "Does that really help?"

"Yeah. It sure as hell does." It was all he could do to think of something more to say. "It...yeah."

That's all he could come up with, lying next to her, her body warm and drowsy with sleep. It didn't feel like the right time for a lot of talk.

Her lips opened, then closed, as if she'd changed her mind about something. And then her voice came to him, soft and clear as sunlight.

"Show me."

Chapter Thirteen

Show her! Had she gone loco? He'd bet his next bounty money she didn't know what she was asking. Sage West might be a good doctor, but she knew next to nothing about the ways of a man and a woman.

She gazed at him without blinking, just waited with what he'd come to recognize as her yes-or-no look. He was trapped. Worse, he was tempted.

He moved his gaze down her torso, lingering on the place where her thighs joined. He couldn't do it. He wanted to, but even a randy loner had rules. One, he didn't bed other men's wives, no matter how tempting the offer. And two, he didn't take virgins.

Besides, "Show me" wasn't exactly an invitation, it was more like a challenge or a request, like "Teach me to rope a mustang" or "Help me improve my marksmanship." Sage wasn't begging. She was just tired and shaken, and needed comfort. She didn't know exactly what she wanted, but he could understand the appeal of another pleasure lesson to ease her troubled spirit.

The problem was, that particular lesson was one he couldn't—wouldn't—deliver under the circumstances.

But there is one thing you could do.

Oh, Lord. She might not like it. But if she did, she'd have the knowledge for the rest of her life. It was a gift he could give her. If she was willing.

Hell and damn, he was growing hard just thinking about it.

"Don't move," he said. Surprised at how hoarse his voice sounded, he cleared his throat. "Just lie still."

Slowly he drew the covering blanket away, letting the bright sunlight wash over her body.

"Feel good?"

"Yes. Feels nice," she murmured. "Warm all over, even my knees."

"Take off the rest of your clothes." He wanted to do it for her, but he didn't dare touch her yet. As it was, he knew he'd have a hard time holding himself back at the end.

"Socks, too?"

He cleared his throat again. "Yeah."

She sat up, unbuttoned her lace-trimmed chemise and let it drop off her shoulders, then wriggled out of her underdrawers. Her lack of modesty was another surprise, until he remembered she was a physician. She'd seen hundreds, maybe thousands, of bodies; she was refreshingly accepting of her own naked state and not shocked by his. In fact, she studied his erection with clinical interest.

Yep, she was a doctor right down to her bare pink toes.

She stretched out her body in the hot sunshine, raising her arms over her head and arching like a sated cat. In that moment Cord knew he was in trouble. Big trouble.

He smothered a groan. She was making it very tough to remember that second rule.

His groin tightened and an ache spread below his belly.

"Close your eyes," he ordered.

"You're embarrassed," she said, a hint of amusement in her voice. "You don't want me to look at your penis?"

Cord shifted on the blanket. "Later. Right now, don't look at anything, just feel."

"All right," she agreed. "But," she added, "it is a very nice penis."

Lord help me. In all the years since he'd grown to manhood, he'd never had a conversation with a woman like this one.

"Now what?" She spoke the words under her breath.

Cord put his fingers on her bare shoulder. "I'm going to show you something."

He smoothed his hands slowly over her body, moving from her chin to her rib cage, her belly, down her thighs to her ankles, even her toes. He did it once more, then again, even more slowly. Under his fingers her skin warmed, and he could feel the muscles in her shoulders and stomach begin to relax.

Finally, he brought one hand to her small, pointed breast and cupped it, brushing his thumb over the rose-brown nipple. She drew in a long, slow breath and released it in a sigh.

"You like that?" he whispered.

She nodded, eyes still shut.

"How about this?" He flicked one finger in a lazy rhythm back and forth across the soft bud. Her sharp inhalation told him everything he needed to know.

"And this?" He bent forward, drew his tongue in a narrowing circle over the warm flesh.

Her breath quickened, and Cord smiled. His own body ached for completion, but it didn't matter; what did matter was Sage's pleasure. He licked the hardening nipple, then closed his lips over the tip and sucked gently. When she moaned, he moved to her other breast and began again. *Lord, he was enjoying this as much as Sage was.*

Nothing had ever felt so good before. The sun beating down on his bare back was nothing compared to this. Her skin was heated and silky under his mouth, and a faint female scent clung to her, a combination of wild thyme and wet meadow grass. She arched upward, bringing her breasts higher, closer to his seeking tongue.

Yes. She wanted more. *Oh, God, yes.*

His own breathing grew irregular. While he licked one breast he circled his fingertip on the other, then moved his hand down over the swell of her stomach to the soft dark hair between her thighs. Her breath caught for an instant, then resumed, the sound dry and uneven.

He slipped one finger inside her. Lifting his lips from her breast, he sought her mouth, soft and yielding, her tongue hot. Shy at first, then bold. Hungry.

"Sage," he murmured. She was wet. Ready.

"Don't stop," she breathed. "Don't st—"

He moved his finger inside her, and she made a sound against his lips. "That's it," he encouraged. "Just let go, Sage. Let go."

"Kiss me, Cord. It feels so wonderful. Kiss me. *Kiss me.*"

He bent lower, brushing his lips over her skin, tasting salt and sweet together, until he brought his mouth to her female center. Her soft cries rose into the hushed morning; his breathing grew heavy and erratic. With his tongue he flicked and teased and probed while she writhed, opening her legs, then raising one knee to allow him greater access. Her fists clenched and unclenched at her sides. Watching her hands move like that almost shattered his control.

He wanted to prolong it for her, but he couldn't handle much more. He fought the impulse to drag her pliant body under him and plunge deep within her. He swirled his tongue against the small, hard bud of her womanhood and at the same time gradually pushed one finger into her entrance and beyond, very slowly, until it was fully inside her. She had no maidenhead.

A knife edge of male jealousy coursed through him until he realized it was probably because she'd ridden horses all her life. She'd never taken a man inside her; that much he knew.

He moved his finger provocatively, then felt her slick passage walls squeeze convulsively around it, pulsing again and again while he tongued her inner lips.

She gasped, arched her back, then went still, her mouth opening in delight.

"Good," he whispered. "It's supposed to be like that."

She moaned a response he didn't comprehend, then lay quiet while he withdrew his finger, curved his hand over her mound and kissed and stroked her belly.

At last she opened her eyes, and he touched himself deliberately. "There's another way, too. And don't say 'Show me,' Sage, because I'm more than halfway there now and you're going to be sore enough."

She stretched both arms toward him, encircled his neck and pulled his face close. "Thank you." The whispered words brushed his cheek. "I think you are…beautiful. I want to watch you."

Cord's breath hitched. *Watch him? Lord in heaven.*

He closed his hand over himself and in three quick strokes spilled his seed onto the ground.

She touched him with her forefinger, then brought it to her lips. Then without a word, she pulled his quivering body close, pressing the engorged tips of her breasts to his chest.

Cord wrapped both arms around her and rested his chin against her forehead, listening to their ragged breathing gradually slow and steady.

He had almost drifted into sleep when he heard the dry click of a revolver hammer.

Chapter Fourteen

Instantly Cord rolled over, covering Sage's body with his.

"I haf you in my sights, Señor Lawson. It ees a very pleasant picture, you and the lady."

Cord swore under his breath. "What do you want, Suarez?" His gun lay under the blanket beneath them. He might reach it by moving his left hand....

"*Nada, señor.* At the moment. Just to look at the lady is enough. She is *muy* beauti—"

Cord's shot stopped the outlaw in midsentence, but he didn't know if he'd hit Suarez. He breathed in the scent of hot metal and gunpowder.

If he'd killed him, there'd be more noise from the salal thicket where he was hidden. If he hadn't killed him, the outlaw could shoot back. He folded his left arm to protect Sage's head.

"Suarez?"

After a long silence, a muffled voice responded. *"Sí, señor?"*

Cord lowered the revolver. The voice was farther away, moving down the mountain out of range. The outlaw was wounded maybe, but not dead.

"Suarez?" he shouted.

"You will pay for this," came a faint call. "And the pretty lady, too."

Cord rolled off her. "Get to the horses," he ordered.

"Fast."

Sage grabbed her sun-dried garments off the tree branch, shoved her trembling legs into her riding skirt and pulled on her boots and shirt. Stuffing her undergarments into the pocket of her jacket, she raced for the mare Cord was saddling.

Without a word, he boosted her up and slapped the animal's rump. "Head cross-country. Stay off anything that looks like a trail. I'll be right behind you."

She guided the horse into the trees, heard his mare pounding just behind her.

"There's an old Indian path about a mile farther on, if I can still find it. It's rough, but at least Suarez won't know about it.''

''What makes you think so?'' Afraid to raise her voice, she half whispered the question as Cord took the lead.

''He's Mexican, not Indian. Superstitious about shortcuts.'' He plunged deeper into the brush.

''Nobody's been through here in a while,'' he called. ''Keep your head down.''

Just as his voice drifted back to her, a vine maple branch slapped at her face. The mare shied, then came to a complete halt. Sage kicked her into motion, but the going was slow.

Blackberry bushes scratched her arms, and the thick undergrowth formed an impenetrable barrier. A broken salal branch told her which way Cord had gone. She kicked the mare again. She didn't want to lose him.

That thought struck her square in the solar plexus. *Lose him!* She wanted to be as close as his back pocket for the rest of her life.

Closer.

Never before had she enjoyed the fact that she merely existed. He had shown her the way, and she wanted it—him—always.

Always. The horse stumbled.

What in heaven's name was she thinking?

Cord wasn't an "always" man. He wasn't even a man she knew very well.

But all the same, she knew things about him.

He was a hard man, but his hands were gentle.

He was a loner and followed no man's ethic but his own.

But he was a good man. Fair-minded and truthful.

He was footloose. A wanderer.

For that, she had no answer. A woman didn't tie down a man like that.

Instead, a woman—if she was intelligent—learned from such a man. Enjoyed what he offered, and in the end, let him go.

She watched his strong shoulders twist clear of a jutting ponderosa pine limb, admired the ease with which he guided his horse through the tangle of salal and maples. Nothing stopped him, and he never broke step.

That was how it would be, she reasoned. At the end of their journey into the wilderness, he would ride away from her without a backward glance.

She didn't care, she decided. If that was this man's way, she would grasp what she could of the moments left and be the richer for it all the rest of her days. The way he made her feel inside, the wondrous sensations he aroused in her, would be enough. What was it he said? *Life is short, feast while you can.*

And so she would. Already her strengthened spirits soared. Her body felt swollen and drowsy with pleasure. *I would follow him anywhere for another taste of that ecstasy.*

As he probed deeper into the forest, Cord tried to put himself in Suarez's boots. What would he do next? If the outlaw had taken a bullet, would he back off? Ride out of the wilderness for help?

Not unless he wanted to save his own skin more than he feared capture. Going for a doctor would tip his hand, reveal his whereabouts.

If I were in Suarez's position, what would I want?

The answer came in a heartbeat. Revenge.

Suarez had accidentally shot a woman who had meant something to him. Cord had forced the showdown, and Suarez had gotten careless. If Cord knew anything about outlaws from his years of bringing them in hog-tied on the back of a horse, it was that they never considered themselves to be in the wrong. If somebody got killed, it was always the other man's fault, no matter who pulled the trigger.

One reason he hated men like Antonio Suarez, men like Zack Beeler, who'd raised him and then turned into a killer, was their arrogance. Suarez and Beeler thought they were above the law.

Above the law. Cord snorted inwardly. The world would crumble into chaos if there were no law, no underlying morality to anything a man did. And if that happened, no one would be safe. Cord couldn't abide that prospect.

The probability that Suarez would want revenge forced him to think. Unless the outlaw was badly wounded, he wouldn't ride out of these mountains without getting even.

Cord stopped breathing. Even if he *was* badly wounded, maybe bleeding to death from a wound he couldn't treat himself, Suarez would still crave revenge.

He would still come after them. Himself and Sage. Suarez would track them or lay an ambush or…God only knew what. But something. Deep in his bones Cord knew Suarez would do *something.*

The question was what?

And the next question was when?

By the time Cord stumbled onto the faint Indian trail he'd been seeking, it was near sundown. The overgrown, pine-needle-strewn path had been unused for years—a good sign—but the fading light made it hard to follow.

His unshaved cheek stung where a blackberry vine had slapped him; looking back, he saw that Sage hadn't fared much better. The sleeves of her red plaid shirt showed small tears where prickly salal and huckleberry had scraped across her body.

He hated to think of anything sharp or uncomfortable touching her skin. He wished he could protect her from all of this, especially from Suarez. By nightfall she'd be hungry and saddlesore, but they'd have to keep moving.

He hadn't heard a sound from her for hours. The realization brought a wry smile to his cracked lips. She'd keel over before she would complain. Fall out of the saddle before she'd ask for a rest.

Jupiter, he wished he'd never dragged her into this mess.

On the other hand, how did he know she'd turn out to be so—so…hell, what *was* it about her? She had backbone, yes. Grit and stamina. So did a lot of people. But Sage, well, she was just…different. He'd never known a woman like her.

He squinted, peering into the thick brush. He should be focusing all his attention on getting

Suarez before the outlaw got them. On earning and collecting his bounty money. Instead, he kept one eye peeled for any sign of the Mexican's presence, and the other eye on Sage.

The situation was not good. Caring about someone on the trail with him made Cord less effective at tracking. Made him take defensive moves rather than offensive ones. Made him vulnerable.

At the thought, he grunted. Hell, it made them both vulnerable, and he was the one responsible for the whole shebang. If Nita hadn't come to the cabin, Suarez wouldn't have shot her; if she hadn't been wounded, Cord never would have brought Sage into it.

The indistinct path slanted downward at a sharp angle. Easy for Indian hunters in deerskin moccasins, hard on horses. His mare skidded a few feet, regained her balance and shook her head. Cord loosened his hold on the reins. "Okay, girl, you're the boss."

Behind him he heard Sage's horse lose its footing. "You all right?" he called.

There was a long pause, then she answered, "I think so. The horse is tired, though."

"That's why I suggested a mule, remember?"

"I remember." Her voice softened. "I have learned some things since then."

Cord grinned. Oh, boy, had she! The best part had nothing to do with horseback travel. ''Yeah,'' he said dryly.

''Well, I have!'' she retorted. ''Don't you want to know *what* things?'' she demanded, after another lengthy silence.

He wasn't sure. It might be entertaining. Titillating, even, to hear her describe what he'd taught her, especially the intimate things. On the other hand, he knew the first word she uttered would have him hot and hard in a heartbeat, and they had a good ten miles to cover before they dared to stop.

''Tell me just one thing,'' he called. He could handle that much. It might take a mile or two to settle down a hard-on, but at least he'd have something to think about besides where Suarez was and what he might do next.

''Well,'' she began. ''I know you're not going to believe this...'' She gave a soft chuckle of laughter and Cord's throat went dry.

''Try me,'' he managed to say.

''You won't laugh?''

Laugh? Not too damn likely. Explode with need, maybe, but not amusement. ''I won't laugh. Go on, tell me.''

He tried to keep his mind on the trail in front of him, on the mare's efforts to place her hooves in just the right spot so she wouldn't slide. He trusted Sage was doing the same, even if she was thinking about…

"I have learned how to make biscuits with whiskey," she announced.

"Biscuits!" The word flew out of his mouth.

"And also that wet undergarments, when dried on the back of a horse, smell like…horse."

"Stop," Cord ordered. He stifled the guffaws that rolled up from his belly. But his male member couldn't care less about the topics of biscuits and horse smell. His sex hardened anyway, and laughter rolled out of him in spite of his efforts.

"What is so funny?" she asked, enunciating each syllable with a touch of frost in her voice.

"Your recent…education," he said. *And my randy male expectation of what you were going to say.*

"Oh."

Cord smiled at a Steller's jay screeching on a branch above his head, and laid one hand over his crotch. He waited for what she'd say next.

"You thought I would mention the floaty way I felt when you touched my—"

The flesh pulsed under his fingers. Cord coughed and reined up.

This time Sage laughed, a clear, unaffected ripple of delight. "I have also learned," she continued in a composed voice, "that men are a bit vain. They take such pride in their...well, their 'prowess.'"

"And pleasure," Cord interjected when he could speak.

"Oh, yes," she acknowledged, her voice still maddeningly cool. "That, too."

Cord sighed. Then she called his name, and he stopped breathing.

"Cord? How long before we stop? Before we can sleep?"

Her soft voice carried to his ear and from there shot straight to his groin.

The precipitous trail leveled out and eventually joined the well-traveled path Cord had followed on their way up the mountain. The meadows were greener and more lush here, with miner's lettuce and wild rhododendron, and the warm breeze stirred the tall wheat grass into rippling waves. For the last hour the twilight had been fading into shadows, and the world was now a velvety black. He could smell water nearby, knew a spring-fed stream tumbled down the hill. They needed it.

For the last hour, as the sun sank, he had also debated what to do, whether to make camp or keep moving. His empty belly argued for food;

a sixth sense argued differently. Suarez knew this trail. If he was still alive, he'd set a trap for them.

Cord brought his horse to a halt and turned back. "Sage?"

She reined in. Her face lifted, a small pale patch in the blackness. He could barely see the rest of her.

"Yes, Cord?"

"What would you think of riding double?"

"Why?"

"I want to draw Suarez off, just in case he's following us."

"Yes, I see. My horse or yours?"

"Mine. I'll weight your saddlebag with rocks so the tracks will look the same."

"Of course," she murmured. Cord knew she was too exhausted to object or argue. Or maybe she trusted his judgment. A glow of boyish pride swelled inside him until he thought he would float out of the saddle.

He dismounted, lifted her from her horse and set her onto his mare, then emptied her saddlebag and stuffed the contents into his own. He scrounged near the trail for rocks and loaded about a hundred pounds worth into the empty leather receptacle. She didn't weigh much more than a half-bale of hay.

He left the saddle on. He'd pay the liveryman for both the saddle and the horse when he and Sage got back to town.

Provided the ruse worked and they *did* get back to town.

Chapter Fifteen

Cord finished arranging the saddlebags on the mare's back, slapped the animal's rump and watched it amble on down the main trail. Then he carefully stepped his own horse into the creek, brushing away the hoofprints on the bank with a huckleberry branch.

Sage waited for him to mount. He splashed into the water and swung his lean body up behind her, pulled her back against his hard, warm chest. His arms came around her as he reached for the reins, and she closed her eyes.

She felt safe. Protected. Not because he had sent her horse off as a decoy, or because he'd stuffed his revolver in the inside pocket of his deerskin jacket. She knew he would keep her safe because she was beginning to know *him*. It would take a lifetime to understand the inner complexities of Cordell Lawson, and she pitied the woman—women—who would try. There must be myriad females in his world who would test their feminine intuition on this enigmatic mixture of hardened predator and pleasure seeker.

But she wouldn't be one of them.

Not that she didn't have the interest. A more intriguing man she'd never encountered in all her twenty-five years, but...well, she didn't have the time. As the only doctor in Russell's Landing, she would have plenty of mysteries to pursue, medical ones. There wouldn't be enough hours in a day to plumb them all, her fellow physicians back in Philadelphia had warned. Her days and hours would be chock-full, saving lives.

But while she was out here in the wilderness with Cord, there was nothing to stop her...well, investigating another aspect of life—one she would have no chance to explore when she returned to the dedicated professional existence she'd chosen. She sighed and settled her backbone into the curve of Cord's chest.

It felt good. *He* felt good. How could she have lived all these years without knowing how wonderful a man's body felt?

Until this moment, she'd spent all her time

studying things in books, learning about a human being from lectures and seminars. Even during her internship and residency, the focus had always been on other people's bodies, other people's feelings, never hers.

There were so many things she didn't know, things she had never experienced or even thought about. Why, for example, did her insides feel so unsettled, so...tingly when Cord touched her? When she sat, as she did now, with her buttocks pressing against his crotch?

A thousand other questions swirled in her head, teasing her curiosity to the point where she thought she would bubble over, like sarsaparilla on a hot afternoon. She squirmed against him, heard his breath hiss in, and smiled into the darkness.

The horse plodded in the center of the rushing stream, hesitating occasionally to find sure footing, then moving on with a switch of her tail. How simple to be a horse. A mare.

Sage had seen stallions cover mares in her father's remuda and at the Ollesen brothers' stable yard. All the mare had to do was stand there, looking unconcerned. Surely with human beings there was more involved? More mutual interest and feelings?

More...?

She would ask him. Cord's answers were always short and to the point, often more direct than she bargained for. But now she needed that. Time was running out on this part of her education.

And the first thing she wanted to know was…

"What does a man feel when he's with a woman?"

His frame jerked. "With a woman…how? Like we are now? Your spine rubbing against my ribs?"

"N-no. Not exactly."

"Well, what, exactly?" She could hear his breath rasp in and out.

Sage shut her eyes and blurted out the words. "Like this morning, when we were…close to each other. Naked."

Another jerk, and then he chuckled. She felt it all the way to her belly.

"Oh, that kind of 'exactly.' What does *that* feel like?"

"Yes," she murmured. She could scarcely believe she—Sage Martin West—had asked such a question. In polite society, a proper lady would faint dead away at the very thought! Or try to.

"It feels," Cord began, his voice hoarse, "like a big empty space opening up in your gut. Like falling over the edge of a cliff."

"Just from…touching a woman?"

"Yeah," he said quietly.

"Does it—the feeling—get better, or worse?"

"Yeah," he said again. "You sure you want to pursue this conversation?"

"Oh, yes, I am sure. There are things I want very much to know. Things I can't ask my father or Uncle John. Things I can only ask you."

"Why me?" he said near her ear.

"Because everything I know about such feelings so far I have learned from you. Do you mind?"

"This is the goddamnedest conversation I've ever carried on with a woman."

"Do you want to stop?"

He waited a long time before answering, so long that Sage wondered if he was disregarding her query altogether.

"Hell, no, I don't want to stop." He cleared his throat. "Not sure where this is taking us, but it's sure making it easy to stay awake."

"Me, too. I find I am quite excited at the prospect of learning more about this topic."

He groaned, then tightened his arm around her. "It's not a 'topic,' Sage. It's part of being alive. I'm glad you're…" he hesitated, drew in a long breath "…excited."

"Oh, good."

"I'm even more glad," he breathed into her ear, "that we're on horseback."

"Why is that, Cord?"

"Hell's bells, Sage. Can't you guess?"

She thought it over. "Oh. *Oh!*" Her entire body felt as if he'd dropped a hot coal down the front of her shirt. "I see," she said in a shaky voice. "Yes, I do understand. Of course. At least I think I do."

Laughter rumbled up from his chest. "Got any more questions?"

She pressed her lips together, felt a slow heat spread down her legs, all the way to her toes, then spiral back up to her neck. She bent her head forward. Cord's warm breath ruffled the loose hair at her nape.

"Tell me what you want to know," he said quietly.

"I want to know why I feel so strange inside when I'm close to you."

"Strange how?"

"Skittery inside. As if my veins had butter-flies in them instead of blood."

"It's because you're female, Sage. And I'm male."

She digested that information as the horse splashed on down the creek, across a sandbar and into a stretch of rippling shallows. "Horses don't feel that way, do they? Mares, I mean?"

"I don't know about horses. With animals the drive is to mate. It's an instinct, like feeding."

"And with people?"

He hesitated. "Well, now, there's people and then there's People."

"Females, I mean. Women."

Again he hesitated. "Same thing. There are women, and then there are Women. Ladies."

"But we are all female, are we not?"

"Yeah. Some more than others," he added under his breath.

"Then I should think that, under the skin, we all have the same instincts."

"Probably."

"And men? Do they all have the same—"

"Definitely."

"Oh, good. That makes it so much easier, don't you think?"

"Not from where I'm sitting," he grumbled.

"And therefore, it would logically follow that—"

"Whoa there, Sage." He brought his mouth to her ear. "It's not male and female we're talking about here. It's one particular male and one particular female. You and me. So let's be honest."

"All…all right. You told me about your falling-over-a-cliff feeling, and I told you about my butterflies. Are they the same thing?"

"Could be."

"A drive to—to mate?"

"I can't speak for you, Sage. But for me, yes. There's a strong drive to mate."

"What…what do you do when you feel it?"

"Depends on the situation. With some women— Hell, I shouldn't be telling you this!"

"Yes, you should. Please. How else will I know? With some women…" she prompted.

"With some women—most, in fact—it's just pleasure. Like a mare and a stallion. Doesn't mean much. With you…" His voice dropped. "With you, it means something."

A fist squeezed her diaphragm so hard she felt light-headed. That a few words could bring a rush of such heady joy…why, it was almost miraculous. No elixir known to medicine could produce that effect so instantaneously. It was like…well, like that flying sensation she had experienced when Cord had touched her, kissed her. And especially when he had entered her most intimate place.

And it meant something to him! *She* meant something to him!

Dear Lord, she felt as if she would float right off the horse.

"Cord?"

"Yeah?" His voice sounded tentative.

"How long before…"

"Before what? Before we make camp? Another hour."

"No, not just make camp. Before we…"

Cord folded his right arm tight across her middle, pulled her up against him. He inhaled the scent of her hair and tried to think.

"Not until morning. We're both tired. And hungry. Not until we've slept and eaten and slept some more."

He kissed her temple. "Not until the sun's pouring down on us like it did this morning. For now, it's enough to just keep riding."

Chapter Sixteen

Toward morning, Cord found what he was looking for. The cave cut into a rocky hillside had been a bear's den at one time; now it served as another of his hideouts. Or stakeouts, when the need arose.

Sage peered at the dark opening. "You knew this was here," she said in a voice rusty from lack of sleep.

"Yep."

"You know every inch of this wilderness, don't you?"

Cord nodded. "It helps to know the area. Makes tracking easier."

"I see. You chase your quarry into these mountains and then corner them. What about Suarez? Does he know the area?"

"Hope not. He knows the Sangre de Cristos

like the back of his hand, but we're not in Colorado.''

''Does that mean we are safe here?''

''For the moment. Even if Suarez finds the cave, we're safe. Look up.''

Sage craned her neck. ''I don't see anything except trees.''

Again Cord nodded. He'd built the simple tree house forty feet off the ground, in the crotch of a giant whitebark pine. From up there he had a clear view of the cave entrance. He'd captured more than one man on the run by letting him ''find'' the cave while Cord watched, rifle in hand, from his perch in the tree.

He walked the horse to the cave entrance, dismounted and reached for Sage. ''There's food stashed in there—tinned tomatoes, beans, a bit of jerky. Even a can of coffee and some whiskey. You hungry?''

''I'm too tired to feel hungry.''

''We'll sleep first, then. Eat later.''

The instant her feet touched the ground, she headed for the cave on wobbly legs, but Cord blocked her way. ''The horse stays here. We sleep up there.'' He tipped his head toward the wood structure high above them.

''But why?'' Sage's sleepy eyes narrowed. ''Why not use the cave?''

"Because I can't keep watch without staying awake all night. In the tree—" he gestured skyward with his thumb "—we're well-hidden. I don't have to stay awake."

He watched her measure the distance. She'd have to climb, but once she started there were plenty of branches well-spaced for footholds.

"It's easy," he said. "Just don't look down."

Sage propped her hands on her hips and faced him. "Do you realize how many hurdles you've dragged me over since we set out on this trek? First I had to swim all the way across a river. Then there was that awful morning we scraped out the grave for Nita, and now you want me to scramble up that tree like a lumberjack? Well, I can't do it. After a day and a night in the saddle, my legs no longer work."

She stared up at him, an accusing look in her blue-violet eyes. "Besides, the food is in the cave."

"There's food up there, too," Cord said quietly. "Even better, there's a couple of rifles and a corn husk mattress."

Something sparked in her gaze. "A mattress? And maybe I could take a bath? Could we heat some water?"

"Nope. Tomorrow you can use the tin kettle shower I rigged up. When the sun hits the trees in the morning, you'll be glad the water is cool. Gets pretty warm up there.''

''Warm,'' she echoed. Again the light flared in her eyes. ''And your tin kettle? It's up there?''

''Yeah.''

''Will you…I mean, well, will you…watch me?''

He held her gaze for a long time, then moved his hand to touch her cheek. ''Damn right.''

They climbed in tandem, Sage in front, Cord below her in case she slipped. Despite her cramped hands and shaky legs, she managed to keep going until she fancied the pine branches reached all the way to the sky, like Jack's beanstalk. Her mind silly with fatigue, she laughed out loud at the thought.

Then Cord was saying something, but it made no sense and she was too tired to sort it out. Something about how he'd constructed the tree house one summer when he needed to be alone. How he'd never brought anyone here before.

The wood structure felt solid enough, but when Cord swung himself up beside her she wondered if it would buckle under their combined weight. Without a word, he pulled up the rope tied to their bedrolls and his poncho. The horse, with the remaining saddlebag and her medical satchel, was hidden in the cave below.

Sage stretched her tight shoulders. The warm night was still except for the soft *hoo-hoo* of an owl. Cord retrieved a makeshift mattress from its hiding place under the platform; the dry stuffing crackled when he shook it out. This side of the mountain got little rainfall, she remembered.

Cord spread the pallet flat, then laid both blankets on top. Sage took one look at the inviting bed and tipped sideways until her body was horizontal. The rustle of corn husks made her smile.

Cord tugged her boots off. "You want to sleep in your clothes?"

"No. Too hot." Her fingers fumbled with the top shirt button.

Cord finished the job for her, then unbuttoned her riding skirt and slipped it off. *Great jumping scorpions, no underwear.* He'd forgotten there'd been no time to don underclothes during their hurried departure this morning.

It didn't matter. He was too exhausted to even look close, let alone…

He shucked off his jeans and shirt, lowered himself next to her and pressed his chest against her bare back. When he could think clearly, he'd decide what to do about the situation. In the meantime, he'd try not to think at all.

Except for the fact that in your whole life, no one has ever felt so good next to you.

Sage woke to the sounds of birds and splashing water. Eyes closed, she lay still, enjoying the sweet, clean air and the twittering sparrows. The splashing noise was so close she could almost feel the cooling droplets splatter on her sun-heated skin.

In fact, she *did* feel them! She opened her eyes to see Cord standing at the edge of the platform, his face tipped up under a shower of water trickling from the bottom of a large cooking pot. It looked like a soup kettle, hung from wires strung over a sturdy overhead branch. Beside his bare feet sat a battered tin bucket of water.

He faced away from her. Water ran in rivulets through his dark hair, down his muscled shoulders. She watched him, studying his movements under the dribbling shower.

The man obviously enjoyed his body. Enjoyed sensation for its own sake. Cord was teaching her something, not with books and lectures, but simply by being himself. By sharing with her what he knew, what he was. Being alive meant *feeling* things. Everyday things. Pleasurable things.

She shut her eyes tight and tried to think of something else.

The next thing she knew, his warm breath washed against her cheek. "You awake, Sage?"

"No." She heard his soft chuckle and her body tensed.

Her world was shifting because of this man. She wasn't sure she liked it.

"You're frowning," he said.

"I am...thinking."

"Hungry?"

"No."

"Want to shower off? I hauled up an extra bucket of water from the—"

"Yes. No! I...I'm not sure what I want. In the last seven days, everything has turned upside down. I'm not feeling like my usual self."

His voice dropped to a whisper. "I think maybe you are, you're just not sure you want to."

Her eyelids snapped open. "Whatever does that mean?"

He brushed the hair off her forehead. "For years you've defined life as drawing oxygen in and out of a pair of lungs, a heart pumping blood through arteries and veins. Now maybe you see there's more to it. You look at life differently.

You can't go back, and maybe you're scared to go forward.''

''I am not sure I *want* to see things—life—differently.''

''What are you afraid of, Sage?''

''Afraid? I am not afraid. Well, yes, I am. I don't know, exactly.''

''Me?''

''Yes, in a way.''

He bent down, brought his face close to hers, forcing her to look at him. ''What way?''

Sage swallowed. ''It isn't because you are...well, male.'' *He isn't just male, he is* blatantly *male. He revels in it.* His body was beautiful, lean and strong, tanned bronzy-gold right down to his belt line. ''It's something else.''

Something unexplainable and mysterious that drew her to him like a moth to a candle flame. It was *that* she feared. She wasn't sure she could put it into words.

''It's the way you...see things. You make me feel—think—about things in ways I never have before.''

''And that scares you, is that right?''

''Damn right,'' she breathed. Her breath hitched at the profanity. She'd never before used such language. Never.

All at once she knew what it was: she was

changing. Cord was making her face some-thing—something she resisted, but that pulled her forward, anyway.

Herself.

"Had to happen sooner or later," he said softly. "It won't hurt you to grow up, Sage. *I* won't hurt you."

Oh, yes you will.

But at this moment, poised at the edge of the precipice, she didn't care.

He touched her cheek, her shoulder. Then he knelt straddling her, smoothing both hands over her skin from her throat to her thighs, stroking slowly and deliberately down, then back up again until her mouth came open.

"You like that?"

"Yes."

He feathered his palms across her belly. "And this?"

"Yes."

He dipped his fingers into the curls at the juncture of her thighs. "This isn't mating, Sage. This is lovemaking."

"Yes." She arched her back, stretched her arms over her head. "Whatever it is, don't stop."

"Couldn't even if I wanted to."

"Good." She exhaled with a sigh. "It makes

everything feel…bigger. More intense. The sky, the trees, even the quiet.'' She licked her lips and smiled into his darkened eyes. ''I feel so…alive.''

''Admit it, Sage. You never had such a good time as you're having right now.''

''No. I never have.'' *Nor will I ever again.*

He pressed his member into the moist heat at her entrance. ''Do you want more?''

''Yes.'' Her voice trembled. ''I want all of it. All of you.''

He thrust in hard and deep, burying her cry under his mouth, and began to move. She was all silk and heat, tight and wet. He'd have to slow down.

''What are you feeling?'' he said, his tone gravelly. ''Tell me.''

''I feel you inside me. It feels…full. It feels…wonderful.'' Her voice caught in a little hiccup of surprise. ''Like there are explosions happening inside me.''

''Want me to stop?''

''No. Oh, no. It's…it's like flowers bursting open.''

''Come with me, then. Move with me.'' He cupped her bottom, rocked her into his rhythm. She clung to him, gasping. He kissed her breasts, her mouth, until she moaned his name and then cried out. Her face was wet against his lips.

Her movements triggered his own release, but nothing he'd ever experienced before prepared him for what happened next. In ecstasy, or in agony—he couldn't distinguish between the sensations—he felt himself rise out of his body and float into another place, soft and black and welcoming.

It was a place he'd never been before, as if a hot light sucked up everything inside him, milked him of his will and his consciousness until, with a shout of assent, he gave himself up to it.

After a long, long time, he heard her voice.

"I will remember this for the rest of my life."

Chapter Seventeen

When they woke, dappled shade spread a lacy pattern over their naked bodies. With their limbs still tangled, Cord smoothed his hand over her tousled hair, let his fingertips play with the loose waves above her ears while he listened to their slow, steady breathing.

"You ever wonder why you've never done this before?"

Sage laid her small hand over his. "Ladies don't. A woman who wants to keep her reputation doesn't...let herself."

"I've known women—ladies—who've kept their reputations."

Her near-violet eyes widened. "Known in the carnal sense?"

He didn't answer.

"My aunt Cissy says a woman keeping her

reputation intact means a man is keeping his mouth shut.''

"Fair enough. He does if he's a man of honor.''

"I take it you are such a man, then? A gentleman?''

He jerked his head up. "Whoa. I'm not sure I'd go that far. Never thought of myself in that way.''

She reached toward him, combed her fingers through his warm, damp hair. "I think of you in that way, Cord. I always will.''

An expression she'd never seen came over his face.

"I've always shied away from civilized things, wearing proper duds, settling in a town.''

"Have you ever lived in a town?''

"Nope. Don't plan to try. I feel more comfortable closer to the raw side of life. In some ways it's more real.''

She twisted her fingers in his hair, unable to let go. "What do you fear in a town?''

"Don't honestly know. I just feel...different, that's all. Like an outsider.''

"In Russell's Landing I feel like an outsider, too. I never did before. There aren't many women doctors out West.''

He leveled a steady gaze at her. "Did you

decide on being a doctor because *you're* afraid of something?''

''Afraid of what? I'm not afraid of study and hard work and long hours.''

''I don't mean long hours and hard work. Maybe you've never done this—made love with a man—because you were afraid of something.''

She thought for a long minute. ''I'm not afraid of men, if that's what you mean. I'm not even afraid of you, though I was a bit at first.''

''Maybe it's not me, exactly. Maybe it's about what happens when a man and a woman get that close. About letting yourself go. Losing control.''

''I did, didn't I?'' she said, her voice soft.

He gave her a satisfied grin. ''Might even be you're scared you'll like it.'' He laid his forefinger under her chin, tipped her face up and kissed her. ''Or that you'll like me.''

''I do like it.'' She stretched her arms over her head and sighed. ''And I do like you.''

His grin widened. ''Good. We'll spend the day up here and travel tonight. That suit you?''

Sage couldn't help her smile. ''Yes. Oh, Cord, I thought you'd never ask!''

''Don't need to. You've answered for me.'' He touched her breast, moved his hand down to her thigh, and she turned toward him.

This time it was like silk, Sage thought. Slow and smooth, his body filling hers as if they had been made to fit together. When he moved inside her, whispering her name with each thrust, she lost command of her senses, and her physical responses welled up from a hitherto untapped place inside her.

She let herself follow her instincts, let herself moan and cry out. He seemed to like it. His breathing caught, then grew more ragged as she grew bolder, touching him, stroking his skin with her heated fingertips.

What a glorious thing it was, being with him. She'd never thought of ecstasy before, never considered it missing from her existence. Now she knew how much she had lacked.

Her only regret was the fingernail marks she left on his back.

Later, sated and drowsy in the afternoon heat, Sage found herself remembering Cord's words. *Was* she afraid of something? Had she buried herself in studies and her professional duties not so much to sustain life in others but to escape it herself?

She watched Cord's chest rise and fall as he lay beside her. She dreaded tomorrow. Dreaded getting back to town, saying goodbye to him.

She would watch him ride away, out of her life, and then face emptiness.

She liked him. Wanted him. She even…

Oh, God, that was exactly what she must not ask.

She glanced at Cord to find him gazing at her, an odd light in his gray-green eyes. "Maybe I'm the one who's scared, Sage."

Her heart skittered to a halt, then slammed against her rib cage. "What do you mean?"

"I've never been…it's never been like this with a woman before. Kinda makes me—"

He broke off midsentence, listening. Sage heard it, too—a barely audible rustle of shrubbery, then the snap of a twig. Cord brought his mouth to her ear. "Stay down," he intoned. "Whatever happens, don't make a sound."

Another movement was audible below, closer this time. Cord rose and moved to the far side of the shelter. Reaching above his head, he lifted an oilcloth-wrapped object from a notch cut into two crossed branches. A rifle, she realized as he silently unwrapped it. He let the protective cover drop to the platform floor.

Sage lifted her head. *Suarez?* she mouthed.

Cord nodded, then pointed the weapon down at the cave entrance and motioned for her to lie still. Another sound reached them from below.

Cord raised the rifle and took aim. He couldn't see anything yet, just the occasional quiver of a salal branch, but something was there, all right. Something that moved on stealthy feet.

Something about the size of a man.

He waited. Cicadas whined in his ear. His palms grew sweaty, his trigger finger slick against the warm metal.

Make a move, he commanded. *Show yourself.* He peered down through the thick branches, straining his eyes. The breeze twitched a frond of fiddlehead fern back and forth; Cord couldn't take his gaze off it. Then another sound, a soft thump, followed by the sigh of leaves, came from near the cave mouth.

He lowered the gun, blinked the sweat out of his eyes, then sighted along the barrel once more and held his aim steady. He'd fire the instant he had a clear shot, not before.

How the hell had Suarez trailed them? Possibly wounded, to boot. Cord hadn't thought the Mexican was that good a tracker, especially not trailing a horse down the middle of a creek. But desperate men could surprise you. They had before; sooner or later, one would again.

Maybe this one.

He pulled his cheek away from the gun stock

and lifted his head. Even if the outlaw had figured out the rock-laden mare was a decoy, even if he *had* picked up their trail, no one could follow tracks made in a streambed.

So it wasn't Suarez in the brush below. Couldn't be. Cord didn't know how he knew this, but all at once he was dead certain. Might be human, but it wasn't Suarez.

When he re-aimed the rifle, he saw finally what it was.

A seven-point buck stepped into the clearing, and Cord swore under his breath.

The click of lowering the hammer sent the animal bounding off into the woods. For the first time in some minutes, Cord felt his heartbeat return to normal.

Damn, that was close. If he'd shot before he saw his target clearly, he'd have announced their location to the whole mountainside. As it was, the episode signaled a warning. He and Sage couldn't linger any longer.

He rewrapped the gun in its oilcloth sheath and lifted it back to its hiding place. "Suarez is nowhere around."

Sage rose on one elbow. "How do you know?"

"He would have spooked that deer. Come on, let's get moving."

Cord unhooked their clothes from the pine branch above his head and they dressed in silence. When they'd climbed down the tree, Cord reloaded the saddlebag and their bedrolls on the mare picketed inside the cave. After lashing her medical satchel behind the saddle, he mounted and stretched his left arm down for Sage.

He pulled her up into his lap, and for a moment he couldn't move. She was so warm and alive. So...*unexpected.* She slid her right leg over the animal's neck and settled back against him. Cord took up the reins.

"Another ten hours and you'll be home in Russell's Landing. Providing we don't meet any trouble." He kept his tone matter-of-fact.

Sage nodded but didn't answer.

"That's what you want, isn't it?"

"Y-yes. I must return to my medical practice."

"Thought so," he said. "That's what happens when you've got a calling—there's always something pulling at you."

She twisted to look at him. "What about you, Cord? You have a calling, as well."

He didn't respond for a long time. "Yeah, guess I do at that. But I always like to take the long way home. And with you sitting so close I can smell your hair, the longer the better."

"I must get back to Russell's Landing."

"I know."

"I might have a patient who needs me. Or a baby to deliver. Or—" *At least I hope I will.* Essie O'Donnell's child was near term, and there was Friedrich Stryker's stiff knee and…

"Yeah. Just wanted to hold the thought in my mind for a while. As I said before, I don't much like towns."

Cord kicked the mare into a steady walk and splashed into the creek. From here the water flowed down the mountain to Pudding Flat, where wild grass and buckwheat filled a green meadow. A mile or so beyond it, they'd pick up the main trail back to civilization.

Civilization. He detested the word. It stood for everything—family, community obligations— that hog-tied a man tighter than any noose. He needed to come and go as he pleased. Alone.

That was the one thing Zack Beeler had taught him that Cord never forgot: *Don't get attached to anything you can't ride away from.*

He didn't want to think about Sage in that vein. When the time came, he knew what he had to do.

But he sure wished they could take the long way back.

Chapter Eighteen

They reached the edge of Pudding Flat just as the sun was beginning to swell over the treetops. Riding all night, resting the mare every few hours and eating handfuls of ripe blackberries while the animal slurped water from the creek, had left them bone-weary.

The morning air smelled sweet and clean, tinged with sage and wild onion. As they dropped into the heart of the meadow, where the grass was knee-deep, Cord couldn't help wondering exactly where Antonio Suarez was.

A warm, gentle breeze came up, licking his face and ruffling Sage's hair against his neck.

She tipped her head back. Then she deliberately unbuttoned her shirt and spread the fabric wide, letting the soft swirl of air caress her bare chest. Such a simple thing, the wash of air and sunshine across one's skin. It brought such pleasure, such a delicious sense of well-being.

"Feel good?" he murmured in her ear.

"Yes. Truly wonderful. And it smells so—so…"

"Rich?"

"Yes, exactly. It's like the earth under our feet is alive and breathing, just as we are."

"I like hearing you say that. It's a way I've often felt, but never managed to wrap words around. You're a damn unusual woman, Sage."

She nestled her head against his neck. "You are a good teacher."

"You learn fast," he murmured into her ear. He reached around her, splayed his right hand over her breast.

She arched under his fingers, thrusting her nipple against his palm. "I like learning," she said. "I always have. Now more than ever."

He brushed his mouth over the tip of her ear. "When we reach town, it'll be over."

She made no response. Instead, she lifted the reins out of his grasp and brought his hand to her other breast. "We're not there yet."

"It's daylight. Won't be long."

"Slow the horse," she ordered in a low voice. "Cord, what if..."

His fingertips brushed her swelling nipples. "If? If what?"

She drew in a long, slow breath. "If you had another hiding place, say at the far side of the meadow, just where it meets the trees? A spot where no one could find us."

"Grass is nice and deep," he said after a moment.

"No one but a crow flying over our heads could see us."

She raised her arm, curving it over her head until the backs of her fingers touched his cheek. He pressed his lips into her open hand, then lazily drew his tongue across the fleshy part of her palm.

Sage moaned with pleasure. Cord buried his face against her neck, then curled his tongue into the shell of her ear.

"Yes," she breathed.

Without a word, he kicked the mare into a canter.

He took her with skill, letting their hunger for each other's touch drive them to uncharted levels of pleasure. When it was over they lay in one another's arms, unwilling to break the spell, until the sky over their heads lightened to peach and then to a cloudless blue. The air was so still they could hear the mare cropping grass on the other side of the meadow where Cord had tied her. Anyone happening onto the flat would spot the horse first.

Again, Cord thought about Suarez. Hell, maybe he'd hightailed it back to Colorado. Or all the way to Mexico.

But Cord didn't think so. A crawly feeling at the back of his scalp told him they'd meet up pretty soon. But damn, he hoped it wouldn't be today.

He rolled toward Sage, splayed his hand against her lower back and pulled her close.

The last mile into town was the hardest. Not because the trail was indistinct or the mare was tired; the trail was all too clear, which only added to the problem.

Cord found himself noticing little things about Sage to store in his memory—the way she held her head, the way her shoulders began to tense as they approached Russell's Landing. The way her hair and the back of her neck smelled, sweet and clean like warm green grass and crushed mint. Her skin tasted of oranges, a flavor he knew he would never get out of his mind.

He tightened his arm around her. "Your name suits you," he said. "Like a mix of sharp scent and sweet oil."

She laughed. "I always thought my name meant I was wise. Or would be, eventually."

"I think you are. You're a lot wiser now than you were eight days ago, when I was sitting on your front porch wondering how any creature as good-looking as you could possibly be a doctor."

Sage sighed. "That seems a long time ago, Cord. So much has happened, I feel…changed."

"Yeah. I feel different, too."

"Wiser?" she quipped with a smile.

"Nope. More scared."

She jerked upright. "Why, Cordell Lawson, what a liar you are! I've watched you day and night for more than a week and there is nothing, absolutely nothing, that frightens you."

"You're wrong, Sage," he stated. Then he chuckled. "Maybe you're not as smart as I thought."

She sat up even straighter. "Of course I am. I am even *smarter* than you thought!"

"Yeah, guess you're right about that." He

bent his head to kiss her temple, then pulled her back against his chest. "You've seen me unguarded, seen into the core of who I am. No woman I've ever known has gotten that close."

"And that scares you," she observed.

His voice changed. "Not the 'getting close' part as much as the hole I'm going to feel inside when I ride away."

She said nothing. They clopped past the schoolhouse at the edge of town, where a circle of pinafore-clad girls held hands and chanted a sing-song rhyme. *"Mary loves Bobby, but Bobby loves Effie! Effie loves…"*

Cord laughed. "It's not easy, even at that age, is it?"

The mare plodded by the barbershop and the Willamette Hotel before she answered. "Bobby and Mary are only seven years old."

"It starts young, I guess."

"It has to start sometime," she said quietly. "Except for me. For me, it didn't come until now."

When it's too late.

To change the subject she pointed out the run-down building next to the jail. "Look, there's the old sheriff's office."

Cord examined the structure with narrowed eyes.

"Jail looks empty."

"The sheriff's office is, too," she acknowledged. "The last man to occupy it, James Giblin, was killed by his deputy."

"Nice peaceful town," Cord muttered.

"Mostly it is. Sheriff Giblin caught the deputy stealing supplies from the Indian agent in Oakport."

Cord shrugged. "Bobby and Mary on one hand, the sheriff on the other. Love and death. Seems that's all you can count on in life."

Sage was silent. They approached the livery yard at the far edge of town, and suddenly Sage heard her own voice speaking.

"I've learned on this trip that all you can really count on is death. The other thing, love, comes when one least expects it. Or doesn't come at all. It is not a certainty, as death is."

"Don't think about it," Cord cautioned.

"Why?"

"You learn some things the hard way. And most often by then it's too late."

The liveryman looked up at the sound of the mare's footsteps. "Miss Sage! Vas vonderin' ven you'd return."

"Arvo." She gave the tall Norwegian a smile, and the man's large blue eyes shifted to Cord.

He spoke from behind her. "I owe you for the mare." He reached for his shirt pocket.

"Oh my, no," Arvo said. "Ginger came in yesterday. I unloaded all them rocks from the saddlebag, and now she is in her stall. You haf some trouble along the way, looks like."

Sage winced. "You didn't—"

"No, Miss Sage. I didn't say vun tiny vord to your mama. I know better den dat. I tell your papa, though."

Sage swallowed. "And what did Papa say?"

"He say iss okay. Your uncle, the marshal, he knows Mr. Lawson." Arvo tipped his head, sizing up the man mounted behind her.

"Is that true, Cord?" she said in an undertone. "You know my uncle?"

"I've turned a few Mexican bandits over to Major Montgomery."

Arvo turned his gaze away from Cord to her. "You look different, Miss Sage. Thinner, maybe."

"Hard traveling and sparse rations, Arvo." Surreptitiously she snugged her bottom into Cord's crotch. "Next time I travel into the wilderness I will be sure to take more time for nour-ishment along the trail.''

Cord made a soft groaning noise in her ear.

''And,'' the liveryman continued, studying her face, ''you look…softer. Dat's it, softer.''

To that remark, Sage had no response. Even when she felt Cord's quiet chuckle rumble against her back, she could think of nothing to say.

After an awkward silence Cord came to her rescue. ''She's tired out, Mr. Ollesen. I'd best take her on home.'' He tipped his hat.

Arvo raised his hand and grinned. ''She needs a buggy for to make her calls, I t'ink.''

''A buggy's a good idea,'' Cord said when they rode out of the livery yard. ''Be a lot more comfortable than a horse.''

''I can't afford a buggy, Cord. At least not yet. I'd have to set dozens of broken bones and deliver half again that many babies to afford a buggy. A horse is fine for now.''

Cord tightened his arm around her. ''I'd like you to have a buggy.''

They turned down Maple Falls Road in time to see a plump woman in a purple hat swish through a whitewashed front gate.

"Why, Sage! Been out on a picnic, have you?" The woman beamed approvingly.

"Good evening, Mrs. Benbow," Sage responded.

"Oh, yes, it is a good evening. I hope you enjoyed yourself?"

Sage choked down a laugh. "Why, yes, in a way. It was quite…educational." But Mrs. Benbow had scurried up onto her porch and through her front door before Sage could finish her lie.

"Educational?" Cord teased.

"The picnic part. That was lovely and you know it," she murmured.

"Sorry it's over?"

Sage heard the catch in his voice and felt a sudden urge to turn and throw her arms about his neck.

"Yes," she said. "I am."

"I want to kiss you," he whispered. "Touch you. I want it so much I hurt."

"Mrs. Benbow is watching from her parlor window."

"Anyone live at your house besides you?"

"No. But Mrs. Benbow…"

"…is watching," he finished for her, his voice hoarse. "Sage, I have to ride on soon. Before I go…"

"She will watch, Cord. She's the town gossip."

"Can she see into your bedroom?"

"She sees everything. And," Sage added with a sigh, "what she doesn't see, she makes up."

He gave a soft laugh. "Well, that settles it." He reined in the mare. "Slide off. I'll circle around and come in the back way."

"But your horse...?"

"I'll hide it. I want an hour with you, Sage. Just one. I've got something to tell you."

Chapter Nineteen

Something to tell me? What could be left to say except goodbye? A word Sage didn't look forward to hearing.

She opened her front door, then on an impulse pivoted and stood watching Cord's mare disappear down Cottage Road.

An utterly irrelevant feminine thought crossed her mind. In just a few minutes he would be at her back porch, and no one—not even Nelda Benbow—would see him.

She smelled of dust and horse and sweat, and her body was grimy and trail weary from her head to her toes. It hadn't bothered Cord this morning at Pudding Flat, when they'd lingered in each other's arms. But that was hours ago. Now she wanted a bath.

She would undress for him, slowly. Step into

the copper bathtub and spread a frothy film of rose-lemon soap over her entire body. And his. And then...

She thought longingly of her bed upstairs, the soft mattress, the clean, lavender-scented sheets. A jolt of raw hunger drove deep into her belly.

She headed down the hall toward the kitchen to pump a bucket of water for heating. Bending over the cold stove to start the fire, she heard Cord's purposeful tread on the back walkway. Her shaking fingers fanned the flaming match so hard it went out in a puff of acrid smoke. Hurriedly she grabbed another from the box near the stove and scraped it across the roughened iron plate.

She heard him mount the three back steps, heard the screen door wheeze open and clatter shut, and then the plop of her medical satchel and the saddlebag as he dropped them on the porch floor. She lit the wood shavings she'd used for kindling and was straightening to meet him when a large, smelly hand closed over her mouth.

"Say nothing, *señorita*," a voice grated in her ear. "We will let Señor Cord enter."

Suarez. Cold terror washed through her. How could she warn Cord?

The outlaw pressed something hard and cold

behind her ear. "I will pull the trigger if you speak one word." He shoved her forward, then crouched behind the stove.

Cord came through the door, took one look at her and his eyes went hard. "What's wrong?"

"N-nothing. I mean, *caveat,* um, *locus.*" His face changed as he translated her rusty Latin. *Beware the place.* His nostrils flared, but he betrayed no outward surprise.

Keeping his gaze locked with hers, he nodded slowly, then reached out and pulled her into his arms, turning her so their positions were reversed. Now his body shielded hers.

"Show yourself, Suarez. I'm unarmed."

The Mexican rose, his revolver pointed at Cord's chest. "Where is your horse, *señor?*"

"Tied up in an apple orchard down the road. Where's yours?"

"Dead," Suarez snapped. "I had to shoot it."

"Take a fall?"

The man grunted.

"So," Cord said deliberately, "you need a horse."

"I haf been waiting for you."

"What makes you think I'm going to give you my horse, Suarez?"

An odd smile spread across the outlaw's

swarthy face. "Because, Señor Cord, if you do not, I will kill the *señorita*."

Sage jerked, and Cord's arms tightened around her. "And then what?" he said in a quiet voice. "You shoot her, I jump you and it's a draw."

"I will kill you with my second bullet."

"You're not that fast, Suarez. Besides…" he paused for a heartbeat "…my horse means more to me than the *señorita*."

Sage sucked in air, but Cord pressed her head against his shoulder and held her there.

The Mexican looked from Sage to Cord and back to Sage. "I theenk you lie. I watch you in the woods. I see the way you look at her when—"

"I'm a man, Suarez. You know what it's like. You take a woman for pleasure, but it doesn't mean anything." The pressure of his hand on the back of Sage's neck increased.

"*Sí*, I know. But for you, no. You do not take just any woman, or you would have had Juanita, your wife." He spat the word through clenched teeth. "Many times you would have had her. She was young. *Muy bonita*. But no, you did not desire her. That is why she came to me."

Cord said nothing.

"So, *señor*, you lie about the horse. You will

save this woman and I will ride south to Mexico.'' His black eyes glittered with triumph.

"You can try," Cord said. "But there's five thousand dollars on your head. That's a lot of money. Buy a lot of women with five thousand dollars."

"But it is this one that you want, I theenk. Not the money."

Sage could feel the blood pulse under Cord's skin, feel the warmth of his steady hand on the back of her head. *Not the money?* Suddenly she wanted to see his face, but Cord wouldn't let her move.

"You're wrong, Suarez. I'm a bounty hunter. Been a bounty hunter for eighteen years now. That's how I make my living."

She *had* to look at him. That wasn't a lie, it was the truth. The man was exactly what he said he was.

His hand relaxed and she lifted her head to gaze at his impassive face. His expression revealed nothing.

"I like women," Cord continued. "But I don't like towns."

Sage closed her eyes, leaned her forehead against his neck. That was true, as well. He had never said otherwise.

His voice continued to rumble in her ear. "I

like the money, too. Maybe more than I should, but…'' He let the sentence trail off.

Suarez shifted the revolver uneasily and Sage felt Cord's heartbeat jump. Good Lord, they were bargaining over her life as if she were a sack of grain! Tears stung her eyes.

She'd thought Cord was different from other men, that he cared for her. As *Sage,* not just as a female.

But now she knew. To him she *was* just a female. A foolish, foolish female.

Oh, damn him to hell.

''There is another thing, *señor.*'' The Mexican tipped his head toward his arm. ''I carry your bullet in my shoulder. I want the *señorita doctora* to remove it.''

Sage stared at the man slouching beside her stove. ''What if I refuse?''

The outlaw's thin lips spread into a smile. ''If you do not do it, I will kill Señor Cord while you watch.'' He waved the revolver. ''This is another thing I see in the woods—you will not want him to die.''

For an instant she couldn't draw breath. Could she lie convincingly enough to bluff Suarcz out of his proposition? Cord had tried and failed; she had half believed him herself, but Suarez had not backed down. Cord didn't seem to mind gambling with *her* life; was it worth gambling with *his?*

"How long do I have to think it over?" she asked, keeping her voice neutral.

This time Cord was the one who jerked. "Jesus," he said under his breath. "Would you really...?" He tipped her chin up, his gaze boring into hers. "Why, you little hellion," he muttered. "You damn little—"

Suarez laughed until his eyes reddened. "You are two of a kind," he croaked when he could speak. "You deserve each other. Now..." the amusement faded from his face "...let us get on with it."

Keeping the revolver trained on Cord, the Mexican unbuttoned his shirt with one hand and bared his bloody shoulder. "It is hurting bad, *señorita.*"

Sage took one look and shut her eyes. The ragged hole looked dirty and crusted with blood. But she had no choice; she opened her eyes and forced herself to study the wound.

Cord watched her retrieve the black leather bag from the porch, then turn calmly to Suarez and motion him into a straight-backed kitchen chair. She laid two shiny scalpels and another device he couldn't name in the bottom of an enamelware pan, pumped in water at the sink and set the pan on the stove.

Cord started toward the wood box.

"Make no sudden moves, *señor,*" Suarez growled.

Praying that the outlaw wouldn't get nervous and accidentally press the trigger, Cord slowed his motions but kept going. He fed the fire until the water-filled container and the teakettle began to boil. The air in the kitchen grew close and hot. He wanted to strip off his shirt, but the Mexican's eyes followed his every move. Cord didn't dare make an unexplained motion.

Sage rolled her shirtsleeves above her elbows, then stepped to the sink and scrubbed her hands and arms under the pump. She waved them in the stifling air to dry, and Cord caught her eye. He raised one black eyebrow in an unspoken question.

"It's deep," she said. "Going to hurt."

Cord leaned against the door frame and tried to think of a plan that would keep her alive. And himself, if he was lucky. She would dig into the Mexican's flesh with one of those shiny knives; he could only pray that Suarez wouldn't lurch and accidentally squeeze off a shot.

Cord thought about taking the outlaw by surprise, maybe jumping him. It had worked before;

no man ever expected someone in his gun sights to come straight at him with a blood-freezing yell. It might work.

Sage cleaned the skin around the wound with a wet towel while Suarez twisted and cursed. Finally she picked up a scalpel. "Don't move," she ordered.

She sliced into the flesh and probed for the bullet while Suarez struggled to hold still. Sweat dripped into the outlaw's eyes, and the fingers of his free hand worked convulsively against his trouser leg.

Cord thought again about rushing him. Yeah, it might work. But if it didn't, the Mexican would turn his revolver on Sage. Cord couldn't risk it. He'd have to go along with the outlaw's plan, let him take the horse and ride out.

But he knew there would be a price. What kind of reputation would he have when word got out he'd let an outlaw walk away, in order to save a hostage? He'd be finished. Outlaws all over the West would know where his soft underbelly lay, and they would use that knowledge as a bargaining chip they hadn't had before.

Still, given the situation playing out in Sage's kitchen, Cord couldn't allow his professional reputation to enter the equation.

She cut deeper into the man's shoulder, while

he squirmed on the chair seat and swore in Spanish. The revolver tilted, wavered, but the Mexican managed to keep the barrel pointed at Cord.

Sage was flushed and sweating. Cord wondered how she could see straight, as tired as she was. Her hand was steady, but her breathing grew more ragged with every passing minute. Why was it taking so long?

She stopped and turned to him, her eyes resigned. "I can't get it," she said at last. "I can feel the ball, but I can't reach it." She blotted her sleeve against her forehead. "It's too deep."

The outlaw gritted his teeth. "*Señorita,* I hope you are telling the truth. It will go very bad for you if you lie to Antonio Suarez."

Sage stepped back, surgical pliers in hand. "I am a doctor, *señor.* I have sworn to do my best for anyone in need. But even a doctor cannot remove a bullet lodged in a bone."

His face contorted, Suarez uttered an obscenity in a guttural tone. "Thees is my gun arm, *señorita.* You will fix."

"I cannot. The wound will heal, if it is kept clean. It will be stiff and may pain you in cold weather, but—"

"*Madre de Dios!*" He waggled the revolver in her face. "How am I to make a living, eh?

You ever hear of a *bandito* with only one good arm?''

Cord nearly laughed out loud. He and Suarez shared something; maybe all men were the same under the skin—worried about how to survive.

He watched the Mexican's hand twitch as Sage sloshed alcohol into the wound and bound it with strips torn from a clean dish towel. He could do it now—jump him and wrestle the Colt out of his grasp. His muscles tensed.

But Sage was too close. He could risk getting himself shot, but not her.

She finished bandaging the Mexican's shoulder and offered a dipper of water. The more Cord thought about it, the clearer the whole mess got.

Part of him burned for vengeance on the man who'd shot Nita simply because she got in the way. Another part of him felt as if he'd been shoved up against a brick wall. Suarez was going to ride out of Russell's Landing and head south, on Cord's horse.

For the first time in his life, Cord was going to let an outlaw go free without a fight.

Through the window over the sink, he watched dusk fade toward night. Inside the overheated kitchen, the three of them faced each other in the deepening gloom.

What the hell should he do?

Chapter Twenty

"Sage?" A thin, scratchy voice called from the front door. "Yoo-hoo, Sage, honey? Are you home?"

Suarez bolted for the back door, but Cord blocked his way.

"It's Mrs. Benbow," Sage breathed.

"I brought you a nice hot apple pie," the voice continued. "Just thought you might be hungry after your…picnic."

Sage wiped her hands on a towel. "I have to go to the door," she said in an undertone. "If I don't speak to her, there's no telling what tale she will invent."

Cord nodded. Suarez retraced his steps and positioned himself in the doorway leading into the hall, the Colt trained on Sage. "If you move," he snarled to Cord, "I kill her. Go," the outlaw muttered to Sage. "But remember, *señorita,* I will be listening to every word."

She moved down the hallway past the parlor and cracked open the front door.

"How thoughtful of you, Mrs. Benbow." Her voice sounded tight.

Suarez flattened his frame against the wall, keeping the gun leveled at Sage. Cord hesitated, then stepped into the shadows under the stairwell just outside the kitchen. He could do that much for her. His mere presence in Sage's house would spark gossip about her; and if Mrs. Benbow thought Sage was entertaining *two* strange men in her kitchen, the old woman would have more than enough fodder to chew on for months to come.

Sage's words floated back to him on the still evening air. "Oh, that's not necessary, Mrs. Benbow. I usually take my supper alone."

"Very well, child, I shan't stay. I'll just set the pie in your kitchen and—"

"No!"

The older woman's blue eyes sharpened.

"I mean, I am heating water for a bath. It's dreadfully hot in the kitchen, so let me just take the pie and—"

"A bath? On a warm night like this? Sage, you do surprise me sometimes."

"Yes, I'm sure I do. Thank you for the pie, Mrs. Benbow. I will return the pie tin in the morning."

"The pie tin, yes..." The older woman's obvious disappointment made Cord smile. "Very well, dear. In the morning. I'll be watching for you."

Sage lifted the pie out of the woman's hands, gently closed the door and leaned her back against it. She closed her eyes in relief. *As if Cord wasn't enough.* As if *Suarez* wasn't enough. Life had seemed so simple and straightforward before she'd gotten involved in...life.

She headed for the kitchen, the still-warm pie in her hands. Halfway down the hallway she slowed her pace, then stopped altogether. No sound came from the back part of the house. No voices. No footsteps. Nothing. The hair on the back of her neck prickled.

She tiptoed on past the parlor, and when she reached the doorway into the kitchen, she hesitated. Silence.

Was Suarez waiting for her, his gun cocked?

Cautiously she peeked around the corner, half expecting to see the outlaw's revolver jammed under Cord's chin. Worse, maybe he was standing over Cord's body?

Her heart catapulted into her throat. Impossible. She would have heard the shot.

Then where…

A tall figure emerged from the shadowed stairwell.

"Cord! Are you all right?"

He pressed his lips into a thin line before he replied.

"Don't know about 'all right.' I just let a killer ride away on my horse."

In an instant she understood. While she'd been talking to Mrs. Benbow, Suarez had slipped away.

"I couldn't risk…" He hissed air out through clenched teeth. "I let him walk out your back door. It couldn't work any other way."

"Oh, Cord. You were so close to capturing him! You must feel awful."

"Not exactly. More like poleaxed."

She turned away from the odd mix of anger and bewilderment in his eyes. "What will you do now?"

"Go after him."

Something snapped inside her, as if a piece of wire had been pulled taut, heated white-hot and then cut. She thunked the pie down on the counter, her usual logic evaporating in a rush of fear.

"Are you crazy? We're both lucky to be alive, and you want to risk it all over again?"

"Yeah, I do."

"Why?" she spluttered. "Just tell me that. Why?"

Something flickered in the depths of his narrowed eyes. "For one thing," he said, taking time to reach out and turn her toward him, "Suarez is a killer. He could come back."

Sage opened her mouth to object, but the expression on his face stopped her.

"And for another," he continued, "he's got my horse."

A red haze descended over her vision. "Your horse! *Your horse!* Are you telling me—? Cordell Lawson, you get out of my kitchen!"

"Sage…"

"Now," she ordered. "This minute!" She spun away from him and grabbed the broom off its hook. Her hands, her entire body, shook like wind-fluttered leaves, but she managed to hoist the implement and swat at his knees. The only other time she'd been this angry was when…

Oh, no. Oh God, no. She'd gone and lost her heart to this man. This footloose rolling stone of a bounty hunter, who loved his horse so much he wasn't even thinking about *her*.

Cord's hand clamped over the wooden broom

handle and wrested it out of her fingers. His steely voice cut through the crimson fog in her head. "Shut up and listen to me, Sage."

"I've *been* listening to you! From the minute we met I've been listening to you, and look what happened."

He gripped her shoulders with fingers of iron and shook her, hard. "Yeah? What *did* happen? Nine days ago you were a dried-up spinster with no clue what being a woman meant."

"Oh." The air whooshed out of her tight chest. "And now?" She could barely keep her voice steady.

"Now," he snapped, "you're alive. Whether you noticed it or not, I've loved you back to life."

"Oh, I noticed, all right. I think I was happier before. Because…" Despite her resolve, her voice broke. "Because being alive hurts!"

Cord's voice dropped to a whisper. "And as for where it's gotten me…" His fingers tightened on her shoulders.

Her heart stopped. She had never considered what it might have cost Cord.

"Sage. *Sage.*" He shook her once more, but gently this time. "Listen to me. I'm not sorry. I know you are hurting, but I'm not sorry it happened. That's what I wanted to tell you. We've changed each other in some way."

"What way?" She spit out the words to stem the tears that threatened.

"I don't exactly know. I'll have to think about it."

"But you're still going after Suarez."

"Yeah."

She gripped his shirtfront in her two fists. "Well, go then! Say goodbye and get it over with."

"Damn it, Sage…"

"Just go, will you?" She leaned her forehead against his chest.

He tipped her chin up and kissed her until she thought her knees would turn to apple butter, his mouth hungry and possessive.

"I'd give anything to look beautiful at this moment," she whispered against his lips. "So you'd remember me. I wish I had on my peach muslin."

"Glad you don't," he murmured into her hair. "I can hardly stand walking away from you in a flannel shirt and those…" he dropped his gaze to her riding skirt "…newfangled duds."

He looked into her eyes, his mouth twisting oddly. Then he kissed her again, hard, and when he lifted his head she heard his breath catch. When she could think again, he was gone.

The slap of the screen door resonated in her ears. She stood in the middle of her sweltering kitchen, fists clenched, her knees trembling, and stared at the apple pie on the counter. She hadn't even offered him a slice to take with him. She had given him nothing, she realized. Nothing.

And he had given her everything.

She walked to the counter, picked up a spoon and dug a piece out of the very center of the pie. She ate it slowly, savoring the tart-sweet flavor of cinnamon and apple, feeling the texture against her tongue, while tears swelled into the corners of her eyes and dripped down her chin.

Chapter Twenty-One

The next morning, after a halfhearted breakfast of stale toast and Aunt Cissy's blackberry jelly, topped off by the last piece of Mrs. Benbow's apple pie, Sage scrubbed out the pie tin and stepped across the street to the widow's trim, white-painted house to return it. Her neighbor's front door was propped open behind the screen to catch whatever breeze there might be on the hot, still air; Sage had bathed just an hour ago, but already her skin felt sticky. Today would be a scorcher.

She smoothed out a fold in her dark blue skirt and wished like anything she'd worn jeans and a plaid shirt instead of two petticoats and a starched, high-necked blouse. Being a woman in the summertime was a suffocating enterprise!

She tapped at the doorframe. In an instant,

Mrs. Benbow's plump form came into view through the wire mesh.

"Sage, child. My, you're up early. Too hot to sleep last night, wasn't it?"

"Good morning, Mrs. Benbow."

The screen door squawked open, and Mrs. Benbow planted herself in the doorway. "Your eyes look swollen," she said, accusation in her voice. "Exhaustion, I'd guess."

"Actually, I slept quite soundly," Sage lied. "Thank you for the pie." She handed over the tin plate.

"Humph." The older woman snorted. "I know tired when I see it. Traipsing about the countryside for days on end..."

Sage jerked. Mrs. Benbow knew about her trip into the wilderness? Worse, she must know about Cord. No doubt she had seen them leave town together. In her hurry to get to her waiting patient, Sage hadn't stopped to think about how much her neighbor relished gossip.

But, she acknowledged, it would have made no difference. When a physician was needed, nothing else mattered. Still, she wished the woman wasn't so nosy.

Sage decided to try another tactic.

"You are quite right, Mrs. Benbow. I am tired. I haven't been on a picnic at all. I have just returned from a medical call in the mountains to treat a gunshot wound.''

''Oh?'' The woman's bright blue eyes surveyed her like an expectant robin eyeing a worm. ''And?'' she prompted.

Sage drew in a long breath. ''The patient...'' Her throat tightened. ''It was too late. My patient died.''

Mrs. Benbow blinked. ''Oh, my dear, how dreadful. No wonder you look so heartbroken.''

''To be honest...'' Sage began. But she couldn't go on.

''Yes, child? You can tell me all about it.''

Oh, no I can't. Not with Mrs. Benbow's gift for embroidering the truth. But oh, how Sage longed to spill it all out to someone who would just listen and understand.

''To be honest, it was a very difficult journey. I...I learned a great deal about what it means to be a physician.''

And a woman.

She steadied her voice. ''I am afraid I'm still affected by all that has occurred. Please forgive me, Mrs. Benbow, but I feel like taking a long walk this morning instead of chatting.''

Mrs. Benbow laid her dimpled hand on Sage's arm. ''Why, of course you do, dear. You just run along now and pull yourself together.''

Her vision blurring, Sage stumbled down the wide porch steps and marched along Cottage Road toward Thad Naylor's apple orchard. At the corner, where Cottage met the town road, she glanced back to see if Mrs. Benbow was watching.

With relief she saw the older woman scurrying off in the opposite direction, toward town, the ruffled hem of her black sateen kicking up puffs of dust.

Without quite knowing how, Sage found herself at the gray two-story house where she had grown up. Her father sat on the front porch, rocking back and forth in one of the bent willow chairs he'd made after her baby brother's death.

"Hello, Pa."

"'Pa,' is it?" The gray-haired man chuckled. "A week ago it was 'Papa.' I see you've growed up some on your travels." He kept rocking, but his sharp blue eyes never left her face.

Sage plopped her aching body into the other chair and pushed off. The weathered willow creaked rhythmically as they rocked in unison.

"How'dja like the Bear Wilderness?" her father asked.

Sage swallowed. "As a doctor or as a traveler?"

"Either," Billy West replied. "Both."

Sage eyed the man who had raised her, and a comforting warmth flowed into her chest, like soothing dollops of heated honey flowing across her ribs. "I can always tell when you're worried, Papa. Pa."

Billy's cornflower-blue eyes widened in fake innocence. "Howzzat?"

She couldn't help but smile. "You come out on the porch and rock in your chair. You never do that unless there's something on your mind."

"Well, maybe I had somethin' on my mind, honey. Guess I was beginnin' to wonder where you were. You're my own little girl, Sage. Even if you are all growed up with a doctor's certificate 'n all, I don't like thinkin' about you gettin' yer elbows bumped or skinnin' yer knees."

"Oh, Pa, I don't feel grown up at all. I seem to be doing it all backward. One day I'm a capable, responsible adult, and the next, well, I feel like a scared little girl trying to climb back on a horse that bucked me off."

"Uh-huh."

"Now I don't even know if I'm a real doctor."

"Uh-huh. Lost yer patient, didja?" Billy said in an even voice.

Sage nodded. Unable to stop her tears, she lowered her head so her father wouldn't see them. Grown-up doctors didn't cry over their patients. At least not in front of their fathers.

Billy patted her hand with his warm, gnarled fingers. "What else happened, honey-girl?" His gentle voice was full of concern.

Sage gulped. "Is Mama inside?"

"Nope. Gone to her sister's for the day. Somethin' about a dress for the church social."

"Good," Sage breathed. "About what else…well, I am afraid I have done something very foolish."

"T'aint like you to be foolish, Sage. Mistaken, maybe. Misguided. But not flighty nor foolhardy, neither."

Sage swallowed. "Something happened in the wilderness."

Billy kept rocking. "That so?" he said quietly.

"Yes. At first it made me happy. Very happy. *Extremely* happy. But now that it's over…"

"Lost yer heart, didja, honey-girl?"

"Oh, Pa. Yes, I guess I did. And it feels just awful."

Billy chuckled. "Well now, I've been there myself, with my heart jumpin' out of my pocket. And you're right, it does feel awful. For a while. After that, you figger you're either gonna live or die one way or t'other, so you just pray a lot and do what you can to make it come right.''

He looked off to the purple hills in the distance, his eyes misting. ''Sometimes a man gets lucky, like I did with yer mama.''

''Pa?''

He didn't answer for a long minute. ''Yes, honey? You got more to say about Cordell Lawson?''

''I—I think I made a big mistake.''

''About lovin' him?''

''No. About running him off in a temper the way I did. He's not coming back.''

''Well, now, I know about Mr. Lawson. Seems your uncle had some dealin's with him awhile back.''

''Yes, Cord told me.''

''What's plain as the comb on a rooster is that Cord Lawson's never been run off by anybody. If he wants to come back, he will.''

Sage's heart stuttered into an irregular rhythm.

''And if he doesn't…well, then, he won't.''

Her heartbeat stopped altogether. ''Oh, Pa, what shall I do?''

Billy halted the rocker with a boot planted on the porch planks. ''Do? Why, hell's silver bells, Sage, nuthin' you can do but go on 'bout yer daily business. Do yer doctorin', and wait and see."

"Wait and see," she echoed. "That's harder for me than medical college!"

"And…" Billy resumed rocking "…you might want to talk to your aunt Constance. Not yer mama—Aunt Constance. Yer ma would have a conniption fit if she knew what you've been up to, and the next thing'd be a posse out after the man. You don't want him hog-tied, honey."

"No. I just want him to care for me. And, well, I want him to…to want to be here, in Russell's Landing. With me."

"That's askin' a lot of a wanderin' man, wantin' him to give up his old life."

"That's what hurts the most, Pa. He does care for me, at least I think he does. But not enough."

"Then there's somethin' you have to decide, honey-girl. You might have to give up a little something to have what you want."

Give up something? She'd worked too hard, fought too long against the entrenched male opposition she'd encountered as a female at medical college to give up even one hour of practicing her profession. Anyway, she needn't agonize over the matter; Cord wanted to catch Antonio

Suarez more than he wanted her. She needn't tear herself into ribbons over a man who'd already ridden out of her life.

She would visit Aunt Constance tomorrow, when Mama wouldn't be there. Sage would pour out her heart to her mother's sister and then she would drink the sweetened chamomile tea her aunt would offer, lick her wounds and take up the reins of her life. Her *chosen* life.

She almost smiled. Then she would go back to her quiet house on Maple Falls Road, and she'd scour that man out of her heart and soul if it was the last thing she ever did.

On Sunday afternoon, she found Aunt Constance, whom Sage and her mother called Cissy, out in her garden, pruning shears in one hand and an oversize egg basket in the other. A floppy sun hat drooped over her face and neck; never in Sage's twenty-five years had she seen Aunt Cissy without a frayed, sun-bleached bonnet of some sort. With her gored skirt rucked up and stuffed into her waistband, her collar unbuttoned, wide muslin sleeves flapping, her aunt looked like a flower herself as she gathered the huge golden sunflowers that covered the front field.

"Good morning, Aunt Cissy."

The sun hat fluttered as the slim woman spun about and came toward her. "Sage! My stars, I'm so glad to see you—you're just in time!"

Sage wrapped her arms around her aunt's slight form. "In time for what?"

"Your mother and I laid out my dress pattern yesterday afternoon, the one for the social? Now I can't bring myself to cut into the fabric. I meant to save it for a shirt for John and another for Matt."

"Mama's usually right about dress patterns," Sage offered. "I'll help you cut it out, if…if you'll give me some advice."

Constance clunked the shears into the flower basket. "Advice! From me? Sage, not since you were four years old has anyone—not even your father—been able to offer you advice!" She narrowed her hazel-green eyes. "What's wrong? Is someone sick? Your mother?"

"No, Aunt. No one is sick."

A thoughtful expression crossed her aunt's face. "It's that bounty hunter, Mr. Lawson, isn't it? I had a feeling about him when John told me."

Sage lifted the cutting shears out of the basket and snipped off a nodding sunflower. "What kind of feeling?"

"Oh, just a 'noticing' kind of feeling." Constance held out the basket for the yellow bloom.

Sage stretched up to cut another. "Aunt Cissy, what do you do when you love someone?"

"Do? You mean as in kiss or not kiss?" her aunt said with a smile.

"I mean, how was it with you and Uncle John?"

"Oh, I see. As in marry or not marry." Her smile widened. "Well, you deserve to know some things, I suppose."

"Aunt Cissy, can I talk to you? I mean, really talk to you? About…things?"

Her aunt hugged her. "We can talk woman to woman. You've earned the right." She held Sage at arm's length, her eyes alight. "Dear Sage, after all your years of hard work and study, you are at last beginning to bloom."

"I don't *want* to bloom. I don't want to change at all. I feel unsure of myself, and that's not like me."

Her aunt nodded, pressing her lips together.

"And I feel jittery and I fly off the handle. I *never* did that when I was young."

"You were never young, Sage. You were well-behaved and sensible before you were twelve. I used to worry about it."

"You did? I thought young ladies were supposed to be well-behaved and sensible?"

"Up to a point, dear."

"Now I feel all wrong and upside down and giddy and not sensible in the least. I feel like one of Mama's baby chicks before they get feathers—all helpless and exposed and not quite right, somehow."

Her aunt Constance laughed and opened her arms. "I think the new Sage is *just* right. Now, my dear one, let's put these flowers in a bucket of water and have some tea. And then I will tell you what I know about men."

Chapter Twenty-Two

Cord kept his eyes on the mud-splattered gray gelding on the other side of the grove of palo verde trees. The saddle sat slightly askew on the animal, as if the rider had bolted before tightening the cinch.

It was early yet. He would wait.

He twisted to study his cover. Suarez could hide in the tamarisk and ambush him, but he'd have to get past the trees to do it. Cord took off his hat, hung it on a cottonwood spur a few yards away.

By noon, noise from the cicadas pounded in his ears like cannon fire. He had to find Suarez. If he didn't, there would always be the chance the Mexican would head north to Oregon again. To Sage. *Even if Suarez manages to kill me, he'll still go after Sage.* She'd be the only one who could testify against him.

Cord thought about that broom she'd swatted him with, and had to smile. Tired as she'd been, sweaty with the heat and the strain of fishing for a bullet in an outlaw's shoulder, she still had the gumption to get mad at him.

His grin broadened. He was glad in a funny way. A woman in love was as quick to kindle as a dry haystack struck by lightning. The thought made a place inside him ache.

And then he heard the footstep behind him.

Constance set the brimming cup of tea on the table. "You see, Sage, I knew I would love your uncle John all my life, whether we married or not. So that was simply that." She pushed the plate of walnut cookies closer to her niece.

Sage had always loved the sunny yellow kitchen with its flowered curtains and polished wood floor. She sipped her sweetened chamomile tea and thought how to phrase the question uppermost in her mind.

"What was what? You mean you didn't care if he went away?"

"Oh, I cared, all right. But when I realized that I loved him, it simplified things. Then I knew what I wanted. I wanted him to come back.''

Sage held her breath. ''What did you do then?''

A soft glow came into her aunt's face. ''I made sure he would want to come back.''

''What if Cord doesn't want to come back?''

Her aunt's dark eyebrows lifted. ''Well, what if he doesn't? It will hurt, of course. But no one can stop you from loving someone. No one, not even yourself. Not even if you wanted to. It's what you *do* about it that will matter.''

''What *I* do? Isn't it something *he* has to do?''

''You cannot simply make other people, especially a man, do what you want. You can do only what *you* want.''

''Aunt Cissy, I want to practice medicine. I want to be a doctor. A *good* doctor.''

''And Mr. Lawson has a calling, as well,'' her aunt reminded her.

''Yes.''

''And you love him.''

''Yes. But...I want him to love me back.''

''How do you know he doesn't?''

''Because he would have stayed in Russell's Landing, but he didn't. He went kiting off to catch that outlaw.''

''That is his life, Sage. His livelihood.''

"If he loved me, he would at least have told me so before he left. Wouldn't he?"

Constance shook her head and smiled. "With a man it is often not what he says, but what he *doesn't* say. A woman learns to read the silences."

Sage gave a small groan and bit into a cookie. "Anatomy textbooks and surgical procedures are easy to understand, but this? Men? Relationships? This is beyond me."

Aunt Cissy refilled her cup, added milk and a lump of sugar and waited. Suddenly Sage was blinking back tears.

"Oh, I do hate not understanding things!"

Constance laughed, then leaned forward and cupped Sage's face between her two hands. "Dr. West? You're a graduated physician, but as a woman you're just beginning your education. Have another cookie and come see me tomorrow."

Sage rose from the swivel chair behind the desk in her office and paced twice around the blue-wallpapered room. Until yesterday it had been the second parlor of the house Mama and Pa had given her as a graduation gift; today it felt like a prison. She could not sit quietly for one more minute, waiting for a patient to arrive!

The hall clock struck ten. Her consulting hours were clearly painted on the neat sign just above the brass door knocker; she'd been waiting a whole hour with nothing to do but arrange and rearrange her shelf of medical books and the journals stacked on the corner of her oak desk. Twice she had flicked her feather duster over the vase of fragrant yellow roses and the fluted glass candy dish, and then she'd reinspected the beveled glass cabinet that held her instrument case and other supplies—not because any dust had settled in the last fifteen minutes, but because she needed something to do.

Oh, why didn't someone—anyone—arrive for a medical consultation? Then she would turn into a whirlwind of helpful activity, gathering bandages or administering medicine or perhaps even setting and plastering a broken limb. She could hardly wait. Her hands itched to be doing something useful, not brushing unseen dust motes off her already spotless supplies.

By noon, her first day as a physician in residence seemed the longest she'd ever endured. By two o'clock, when she decided to forgo even a light lunch in case a patient happened by, she simply could not believe that no one, *not one soul* in Russell's Landing, had a sniffle or a sore shoulder or something that needed treatment.

Her fees were reasonable; she'd made it known she would accept eggs or bushels of corn in payment. She was well-qualified and extremely capable. *So why has no one knocked at my door?*

Had word spread about her failure to save that young Mexican girl in the mountains? Sage thought it over, then decided that wasn't the case. In Russell's Landing, gossip spread like ball lightning rolling along the hilltops. If the townspeople knew something, it was instantly, and loudly, on everyone's lips.

She plunked herself back down on the cane-bottom office chair, propped her elbows on the smooth oak desktop and leaned her forehead against her folded hands. *What good am I as a doctor if I have no patients?*

She considered the question so intently she failed to hear the *rap-tap* at the front door.

The sharp knocking sounded again, and Sage raised her head. What was that noise?

Rap-bam! Someone's fist battered the plank frame.

"Dr. West? Sage?"

Oh, please let it be Cord. Please, Lord.

She flew down the hall and flung open the door, then felt as if a pail of stones spilled over in her stomach.

"Why, Mr. Stryker, good morning! What can I do for you?" Her heart thudded so loudly she almost missed his answer.

"Good afternoon. I came to—"

"Of course, Mr. Stryker. Come right into my office, won't you?"

A patient! How fitting that it should be her old friend Friedrich Stryker with a medical complaint. She noted the newspaper editor's halting gait as he followed her down the hallway. A sprained ankle, perhaps? Rheumatism?

"Sit right down here," Sage said, gesturing to the carved-back consulting chair positioned alongside her desk. Sure enough, he favored one leg when he seated himself.

"I hope this is no bother, Miss Sa—uh, Dr. West."

"Why, it's no bother at all. It is, after all, what I am trained to do."

An unsettled look crossed his craggy face. "Trained?"

"Of course," she said, trying to keep that note of pride out of her voice. She'd spent six years preparing for this moment. *Be business-like. Professional.*

"And what is the problem, Mr. Stryker?"

"Oh, no problem, Miss...Dr. I just came by to ask..."

"Yes?"

"To ask…that is, to see if you could…"

Sage thought she would explode. "Let me guess. It's your leg, is it not?"

His bushy gray eyebrows rose. "My…?"

"Possibly your ankle? Or a stiff—" She broke off at the frown that brought his eyebrows back down almost to the bridge of his nose.

"I beg your pardon?"

"Mr. Stryker, we will get nowhere if you cannot tell me where it hurts."

The newspaper editor straightened in the hard-backed chair. "Here." He tapped his chest with the knuckles of one hand. "It hurts here, in my heart."

Sage felt the blood drain from her face. "Your heart?" she whispered. "You mean you have pains in your chest?"

"Nein, nein," the man sputtered, shaking his head.

"Not your chest, then. Your arm? Your jaw?"

Friedrich Stryker lurched to a standing position and made an awkward bow from the waist. "I came to…to apologize. To ask you to forgive me for writing that you were…plain. You are not plain, Miss Sage. I wanted to make a point in my editorial, and I was carried away by my rhetoric."

Sage grew a bit dizzy. "You came about…rhetoric?"

"Exaggeration," he amended. "I did not mean…" He sagged into the consulting chair once more.

"But your leg?" Sage said, brushing aside the man's explanation. It was his affliction, not his apology, she wanted to address.

"There is nothing wrong with my leg."

Sage tilted her head back and studied Mr. Stryker's trouser-clad limb. "You favor one leg when you walk," she said. "Your left leg, I would guess. See how you hold it straight when you sit?"

He glanced down at the appendage, attempted to bend it. The effort made him wince.

"Your knee is stiff, is it not?"

"My knee? Oh, well, it is sometimes, a little…. But it is early yet. I have not exercised."

"It is four o'clock in the afternoon, Mr. Stryker. You have a stiff, probably painful knee, and you are here in my office where I conduct my consultations. Shall I take a look?"

"*Himmel!* Look at my leg? Certainly not."

Sage bit back a smile. "It is perfectly proper, Mr. Striker. I am a physician, remember?"

"But…"

"Roll up your trouser leg, please." She kept her voice as crisp and neutral as she could.

"Oh, Miss Sage, I couldn't allow you to—"

"Here," Sage interrupted. "Have a lemon drop." She offered the fluted bowl of candy, and when both his hands were occupied, she bent swiftly and hiked up his pant leg.

"Miss Sage!"

"Dr. West," she corrected in a calm voice. She eased the fabric over the man's smooth white kneecap and heard the crunch of the lemon drop in his mouth.

"It is swollen, here and here." She touched his skin lightly with the tip of a steel probe. "Does it hurt?"

"I—" He swallowed the remains of the lemon drop.

"You must tell me, if I am to help you." She waited while he munched another candy.

"It is stiff in the morning," he said at last. "Before breakfast. After I walk to the newspaper office it pains a bit, yes. I cannot go down my porch steps without it hurts. Here." He tapped his kneecap.

Sage nodded and gave him her best "Mmm-hmm." "How many floors have you in your house, Mr. Stryker?"

"Three. Four, counting the basement."

"Mmm-hmm."

Fear flickered in his tired blue-gray eyes. "You think I am going lame, like an old man?"

"Certainly not," she said in a breezy tone. "You have a touch of rheumatism, and you have aggravated it by going up and down too many stairs of late."

"Oh?" He lifted another lemon drop from the bowl.

"I prescribe a half teaspoon of this powder. It's crushed willow bark, and you must dissolve it in a tumbler of water and drink it morning and evening."

She removed a brown glass bottle from the cabinet, shook a scant handful of the contents onto a square of white parchment and folded it into a packet.

"And…" she added as he hurriedly rolled down his trouser leg, "…try to stay on the first floor of your home for the next week. Let the inflamed tissues heal. I will prepare some special liniment for you and bring it to the newspaper office tomorrow."

Mr. Stryker stood up. "I thank you, Dr. Sage. For your professional opinion." He held out his hand. "And for accepting my apology for what I write in the paper."

Sage enfolded his ink-stained fingers in hers.

"We have always been friends, Mr. Stryker. You used to correct my spelling, remember? Now I am correcting your patellar ligament."

"It is a good bargain. You have learned very much. I will tell Flora about your nice office," he said. "She will like to hear."

"Thank you, Mr. Stryker."

"Also," he said with a twinkle in his watery blue eyes, "I will tell about the lemon drops. That, I think, you learn from me."

Chapter Twenty-Three

Cord swore under his breath. Ambush. Goddamn it, whoever it was had got the jump on him.

"Do not move, Señor Cord."

His gut clenched at the voice. How could he have lost Suarez long enough for the outlaw to circle around in back of him?

"Again I have you in my sights, *señor*. You grow careless."

Cord said nothing. He thought about the distance between his palm and his holstered revolver. He wouldn't have enough time. He hadn't been careless, he'd been tricked. Suarez had laid a false trail.

"You got a new plan, Suarez?"

"Ay, I do. Santa Maria came to me in a dream, and she tell me what to do."

Cord heard the sand crunch as the man took a step forward. Next to his own lengthening shadow in the lowering sun's light loomed a shorter one. Solid and compact, as if the figure was hunched over. As if…

In that instant he knew what Suarez intended to do. The Mexican wouldn't risk shooting him in the back. Too obvious. He'd get Cord to turn around. Either that or…

The shadow changed, spread wide and moved in. Cord bent, clenched his hands together and whirled. His knotted fists caught Suarez's gun arm, just as he raised it to crack the weapon against Cord's skull.

Yeah, he'd been right. Suarez intended to knock him senseless, then shoot him in the chest and make it look like an accident.

The revolver catapulted out of the outlaw's hand, dropped onto the coarse sand with a plopping sound. Before Cord could kick it out of the way, Suarez threw his body on top of it.

"Get up," Cord ordered.

Suarez's hand twitched under his belly. Cord expected it, knew the man would maneuver the revolver into his grasp, then roll over on his back and fire at him.

His hand itched to draw his own weapon and

make an end of it. Taking him alive was better, but at the moment dead seemed very attractive.

"Now!" Cord's voice dropped to a whisper. *"Comprendez?"*

Suddenly Suarez flopped over, his hand scrabbling for the weapon beneath him. The gun went off.

Oh, Jesus. The misaimed bullet punched a hole in the Mexican's neck. Within a heartbeat he lay motionless, eyes open and staring at the sky.

It was over.

A week dragged by. Then another. Sage's spirits rose when the occasional patient stopped in, and fell when her mother came to cluck sympathetically and ask what she was eating that she looked so peaked. Apparently Aunt Cissy had told Mama just enough to calm her worries and her Billy-get-the-shotgun response, but not enough to set her fears entirely at rest. Sage wished her mother would call during office hours; that way, when Mama got sniffly, Sage could escape to an imaginary patient in the reception room.

On Thursday, the *Willamette Valley Voice* was published. Sage had asked Mr. Stryker to print a simple boxed announcement of her office hours. She guessed it had done some good, because by midday, the trickle of patients began to turn into a steady stream.

She was kept so busy with sore throats and sprained ankles she didn't get to sit down and read the paper herself until the following afternoon. At day's end, tired after lancing a boil on Thad Nayler's neck, setting two broken arms at opposite ends of Douglas County and concocting a batch of salve for Mr. Stryker's sore knee, Sage finally sank onto her shaded front porch and unfolded the unread newspaper.

Doctor's Heroism Lauded.

Instantly alert, she scanned the print beneath the headline.

Dr. Sage West has recently returned from a harrowing and dangerous trek into the wilderness on a call of mercy. Accompanied by only an Indian guide...

"Indian guide!" Sage spluttered.

...our intrepid and gallant physician rode day and night, bravely meeting all hazards of the wild with singular courage.

She clapped her hand over her mouth. How fortunate that Mr. Stryker had such good journalistic sense.

And a sore knee. She would take the salve over directly and thank him for his restraint. Knowing Mrs. Benbow, it must have been difficult.

Patients poured in all the next day. Letitia Halstead complained of palpitations from canning forty quarts of snap beans on the hottest day of the year. Arvo Ollesen limped over with a lump on his hip the size of a dishpan where a horse had kicked him. Both the Runyon twins were down with the measles, and after Sage rode out to check on them, she returned long past suppertime to find Rafe Pokell waiting.

"Ella's havin' her baby," he announced.

Sage sighed and climbed back onto the saddled mare and followed him to his farmhouse outside town.

Every hour of the night, and all through the long, hot day as Ella labored, Sage boiled water and murmured encouragement and thought about Cord. Was he alive, or had Suarez killed him somewhere along the trail? Would he be pleased that she was gaining patients? Was he even thinking of her at all?

The baby was born at dusk, a wrinkled but

beautiful boy with a fuzz of dark hair. Rafe cried, and then Ella cried, and then Sage as well, tears streaming down her sweat-sticky cheeks. Then all three of them laughed at themselves and drank a toast of warm milk and whiskey. They named the baby Justin, and Sage rode wearily back to town just as the setting sun turned the sky pink.

She felt good. Tired, yes, but satisfied that she had done her best and it had come out right. This was life itself, she reflected as she guided the horse past the apple orchard. Bringing new life into the world made her feel alive.

And yet…

Down deep inside, in a place so secret most of the time she didn't know it existed, something called to her. Something thrilling and sweet that bit into her heart.

Cord. Oh, Cord.

Chapter Twenty-Four

The annual July social, held in the maple-tree-dotted meadow next to the Methodist Church, brought the community of Russell's Landing together for a midsummer celebration. Farm families came with barefoot children crowded into wagons; townsfolk put on their Sunday best and gathered by the tablecloth-swathed trestle tables to gossip and exchange yarns, speculate on the weather, exclaim over new babies.

By the time Sage arrived with her pies, one lemon and one cherry, the speeches were already under way. Her father, the mayor, stood near the wood platform listening to the speakers, his gold pocket watch ostentatiously displayed. When their time was up, he cut them off with a finger drawn across his throat.

Any citizen who had something to say was

invited to speak his or her piece, and the speeches never lasted very long. Over the years, community dignitaries and housewives alike had learned not to ramble.

Sage made her way toward the already loaded dessert table, overhearing the tail end of Cal Ollesen's announcement about new rates for boarding horses at the livery. "Yus' t'ink you all like to know," Cal finished.

She stopped to hug her father as she passed. Billy squeezed her tightly, but kept one eye on his watch. "You wanna speak about yer office hours, honey-girl?"

"No, Pa. Word seems to be spreading. My patient load is running over."

"Must be that horse kick you doctored on Arvo's hip. Why, he all but gave you a testimonial earlier."

Sage laughed. "I'll bet he didn't tell how he refused to unbuckle his trousers and let me inspect the wound!" She kissed her father's gray-whiskered cheek. "Until I insisted. Men can be such babies at times!"

With a mixture of pride and puzzlement, the mayor looked down at the daughter he had raised. "How do you know so much about men all of a sudden?"

Another speaker started in. "We oughta clean

up the jail, maybe get us a new sheriff.'' Sage recognized the voice as Seth Duquette's. Like his father, Joshua, Seth enjoyed the idea of bullying people.

"Who we gonna put *in* the jail, Seth?'' someone called. "Ain't got much wrongdoing hereabouts 'cept for apple snitchin'.''

"Oh, we got some, all right. Kids runnin' wild after school. Bank robbed over to Dixon Falls last week. I even heard an outlaw was spotted right here in Russell's Landing.''

Sage spun away from the table and caught her father's eye. *Had Antonio Suarez returned?*

"Time!'' the mayor yelled.

"But I ain't finished yet!'' Seth yelped.

"Yes, y'are, son.''

A spatter of applause rippled over the crowd.

"Next, we'll hear from Letitia Halstead. She's gonna share the recipe for her lemon peel cake.''

More applause. Women rummaged in pockets and reticules for paper and pencil.

"Don't want the recipe, Letitia, just give us the cake!''

Everyone laughed until the tiny woman in blue-checked gingham rose and walked forward. "You hush up, Parker Ramsey. Get your wife to bake you one! Now, listen up. Take two handfuls of sugar and a half teacup of butter, and when it crumbles nice, you take and skin four lemons and…''

Sage memorized the recipe as Letitia recited it, but she knew it would not taste the same; Mrs. Halstead always purposely left out one ingredient in her most sought-after dishes.

Sage had to laugh at the foibles of human beings. The townsfolk, and the farm families, too, now that she was paying medical calls and getting to know them, were dear to her heart. Not perfect, just human. Flawed and wonderful. Exasperating and lovable at the same time.

She stepped away from the throng of people now arranging cloths and blankets for their picnics on the lush meadow grass. Moving up a little hillock, she turned to survey the doings.

She loved this place, even if she didn't feel a part of it in some ways. Women her age had grown up and married while Sage was away at medical college. By now, her schoolgirl acquaintances had two or three babies.

Her mother's friends, and Aunt Cissy's, were the hardworking, aproned women who ran the Ladies Aid Society and sat on church committees, the ones who helped raise their grandchildren. Sage supposed she would end up doing the same. Except, she thought with an odd tightening in her throat, she wouldn't have any grand-children.

She gazed down on the families grouped to-gether, the knots of women chattering over a baby's bonneted head, and for an instant her heart split right down the center. Ella Pokell's baby, Arvo's bruised hip, the three new cases of measles in the county—these were the things that mattered to her.

And a blue-eyed baby in a ruffled yellow bon-net?

She couldn't answer that question, any more than she could stop the tears blurring her vision into a kaleidoscope of changing colors and tex-tures.

A speaker's raucous voice cut into her thoughts. "I t'ink we need a hospital!"

"Like hell we do. We need a jail." Seth Du-quette's voice.

"We all need some of Miz Letitia's lemon cake!" her father interjected.

"And some ice cream!" four-year-old Ro-sanna Ramsey piped. "Banilla!"

Four years ago Rosanna was just a dream of Parker Ramsey and his new bride, Natasha Pe-trov, the mercantile owner's daughter from Dixon Falls. Sage's cousin, Matt, had taken one look at the exquisite woman with her dark hair braided into a crown, and fallen in love on the spot. Unfortunately, Matt's glimpse of her had occurred at her wedding to Parker. After that day, Matt rarely looked at a woman.

Until now, Sage could never understand why her cousin was so disinterested in the opposite sex. Now she understood completely. She had no more desire to cast her eyes on a male—even a strong, healthy one—unless he wore a familiar plaid shirt rolled up to his elbows and unbuttoned to the waist to catch the breeze, and torso-hugging jeans with nothing underneath.

Merciful heavens, what a shameless thought!

Yes, indeed, Dr. West, a voice within whispered. *Lately you seem to be feeling as human as the next woman.*

She found herself scanning the crowd for a tall, lean man who moved like a graceful cat stalking its prey. Not one man even remotely resembled Cord Lawson.

She shifted her gaze to the buildings along the main road through town, watching for a telltale puff of dust until her eyes burned.

He would never return. At the bottom of her heart she knew a man like Cordell Lawson preferred to wander. And besides, he'd always said he didn't like towns.

Sage shook the thought out of her head, lifted

her skirt and started down the hill toward Aunt Cissy and Uncle John.

Aunt Cissy looked like a willowy stalk of green corn lily in her new emerald muslin. Uncle John, in a faded blue army shirt and crisp trousers, was still the handsomest man within a hundred miles, but he had eyes for no one but Aunt Cissy. When she looked up into her husband's face, Sage's heart caught. They were beautiful together, even after all these years.

And, Sage noted with a smile, even her mother was acting a little silly this fine July day. Every time Billy spoke, a worshipful look and a blush came over Nettie West's still creamy complexion.

How Sage loved seeing them together.

Oh, damn that Cord Lawson, anyway! She didn't want to miss this mysterious, splendid thing that bound a man and a woman together with such long-lasting but invisible threads. It made her heart ache just to think about it.

The next morning, she met Mrs. Benbow outside Duquette's Mercantile. "Oh, my dear, have you heard?"

Sage took a step back. "Heard what?" She held her breath as Mrs. Benbow slapped her palm against her heaving bosom.

"About the wedding!"

Sage blinked. "What wedding? Who is getting married?"

"Why, the Pokell girl, of course. Sarah's been sweet on Eli Ramsey since she was in pinafores, and now—my stars, isn't it exciting? He proposed last night. Got down on one knee right on her back porch…" The buxom woman paused for breath. "And then she kissed him, and he kissed her, and she started to cry and—"

"Just how do you know all this?" Sage interrupted.

The woman's eyes rounded. "Why, I watched them, of course! The Pokells' porch is just across my back garden."

"Forgive me, Mrs. Benbow, but doesn't that strike you as being a bit…nosy, spying on a courting couple?"

"Why, no, Sage. I've known Sarah for years. Her mother and I are practically sisters, you know. We grew up together, right here in Russell's Landing."

"You are not sisters," Sage corrected. "You and Minerva are first cousins, the same as Matt Montgomery and me. Even so, that doesn't give you the right to—"

"Why, Sage West, I do believe you are jealous."

"Jealous?" Sage snapped her jaw shut. Jealous of Sarah Pokell? The last time Sage had seen Sarah the girl had just won the three-legged race at a summer social, wearing jeans with red patches on the knees.

"That's what I said—jealous. Look at yourself, Sage. You're practically an old—"

"Don't you dare say that!" Sage blurted. "Sarah Pokell cannot be a day over seventeen. What could she possibly know about life? About love?"

"I don't in the least see what age has to do with it. Now, you take Parker Ramsey, why, he was practically an old man when he fell in love with that Russian scamp from Dixon Falls."

"Natasha Petrov was never a scamp!" At the back of her mind, Sage wondered why she was arguing over this. It wasn't as if she and Natasha were friends; she barely knew the woman.

"Gypsy, then. Anyway, she's foreign."

At that, Sage exploded. "Foreign! We are *all* foreign on this soil—that is, unless we're Indian."

Mrs. Benbow's generous bosom swelled with indignation.

"Anyway, the wedding is to be this Sunday," she huffed. "At the church. The Ladies Auxiliary is already baking for the reception, and...oh my, that reminds me, I'm out of cinnamon.'' She veered toward the mercantile entrance. ''I'm making two dozen of my apple tarts.''

''Apple tarts,'' Sage echoed. ''That's nice.'' She turned away. Her anger had evaporated. In its place a hollow yawned beneath her heart. Sarah Pokell and Eli Ramsey, to be married on Sunday. Little Sarah with the scrawny knees would bind her life to a man, would promise to love and honor and obey, for better or worse. *Why, why did this hurt so?*

Clear as a rumble of thunder, she heard her father's low, raspy voice in her head. *Might want to give it some thought, Sage honey. Setting bones and bringing babies doesn't keep a woman warm at night.*

Mrs. Benbow disappeared to the silvery sound of the bell over the mercantile door.

''Oh, yes it will,'' Sage murmured. ''I'm not going to risk my heart for a warm…''

She gulped in air. ''I didn't spend all those years learning how to stitch wounds and deliver babies just to throw it all away on…a male of the species.''

So there.

Chapter Twenty-Five

The Senorita Saloon in Nogales looked as if a dust storm had dumped half the Mexican desert on the floor. Sand crunched under Cord's boots, but his throat was so dry he didn't care.

"Double whiskey," he rasped to the barkeep.

The splash of the amber liquid made his mouth water. Two weeks without rest or a drink, a month without a woman...even his soul felt dry. He slapped his last silver dollar on the scratchy counter.

"Dollar a shot," the chunky bartender said. He scooped up the single coin and thrust out a meaty hand. "You owe me one more, cowboy."

"That's my last one. How 'bout I drink just half?" Cord offered with a smile.

"How 'bout you wipe that grin off yer face

and pay up? You don't look like a feller down to his last dollar.''

"Can't pay you until tomorrow," Cord said slowly, sizing the man up. He didn't want a fight. He was so tired he wasn't sure he could stand up long enough to land a punch, but he was damn desperate for a drink. "How about it?"

"What's so special about tomorrow? It's Sunday. You a Bible beater?"

"Tomorrow I see the federal marshal."

"So?" The barkeep pushed the grit on the counter around with his rag. "What's the marshal got to do with it?"

"He's holding my money," Cord said in a tired voice.

"Yeah? What for?"

"Bounty." He watched the man's rheumy eyes widen.

"Yeah? What for?" the barkeep said again.

"Antonio Suarez. I brought him in an hour ago."

"Jesus! Dead or…?"

"Dead," Cord snapped, "Look, mister, I'm plumb out of good humor. I'm going to drink my whiskey and then I'm going to order another one, a double, so tomorrow my bar bill will be three dollars. Now, take your hand off that glass.''

''You got a name, cowboy?''

''Cordell Lawson.''

The fat fingers spread and lifted away from the shot glass. In the next instant a square quart bottle of Tanner's Red Eye appeared on the counter. ''Drink up, Mr. Lawson.'' The silver dollar slid back across the counter. ''On the house.''

It took four fingers of whiskey to settle Cord's gut and drive the past twenty-five days into the back of his consciousness. He hadn't wanted to kill Suarez. All he'd wanted was to keep him away from Oregon and Sage. Putting him behind bars would have done it, but Suarez had made a mistake staking out that ambush.

Cord had packed his body into Nogales tied onto the back of the gray mare Suarez had taken. *His* gray mare.

He downed another swallow and felt the knot inside him begin to loosen. It was over. The only thing he had to decide now was what he'd do with the money.

More whiskey, for starters. He tipped the bottle forward and refilled his glass.

For the next two hours he tried very hard not to think about Sage or anything that reminded him of her. Sage making biscuits with whiskey. Her white muslin drawers fluttering off the backside of her horse. That day in Pudding Flat when the earth stopped turning as they'd come together.

He drank more than he should have, kept drinking until the sharp hunger in his soul faded to a kind of acceptance.

She wasn't for him. She wasn't available to any man, if he thought about it. She wanted to be a doctor, to diagnose and treat a man, not travel with him.

He remembered that first time, how she'd looked hard at his manhood, even brushed her fingers across the tip and tasted his seed. One hundred percent scientific curiosity.

With a groan, he poured his glass full, leaned his head into his hand and closed his eyes.

He would never forget that day. He'd almost wept, he'd been so moved.

The day Sarah Pokell married Eli Ramsey was a day Sage would remember for the rest of her life. It started like any other Sunday in July, the cloudless sky arching overhead like a sapphire bowl, the morning air sweet with the scent of honeysuckle and Mrs. Benbow's front rose garden.

The church bell tolled at eleven o'clock, just as a wagon rumbled down the street, mother and father toting black, leather-bound Bibles, the children riding in the back, scrubbed and subdued, dressed in their Sunday best.

The small white-painted church would be crammed to the rafters this morning, and most families would stay on for the wedding ceremony later that afternoon.

Sage spent the morning sterilizing instruments and repacking her medical satchel. Only when the hall clock chimed two did she climb the stairs to her bedroom and don the peach muslin, tidy her hair and settle the wide-brimmed straw hat in place.

The afternoon sun heated the back of her neck where the hat didn't shield. By the time she reached the board walkway along Main Street, the hot rays scorched her spine right through the fabric of her dress.

It felt good in a way. Comforting. At the same time, the pleasure of the sensation sent her mind skittering from the steaming scalpels and forceps she'd left on the stove to air dry to picking an armload of Mrs. Benbow's Belle of Portugal blooms to scent the drawers of her chiffarobe. Her patients teased her when the sheet draping her examination table smelled of roses, but she didn't care. It made her feel good.

A thunderstorm threatened. The sultry heat pressed down, driving her into the church an hour ahead of the ceremony, where she slid into an oak pew at the back and tried to settle her thoughts.

What did it mean to marry a man, as Sarah Pokell would do this afternoon? What would a woman have to give up to become someone's wife?

Sarah sewed beautifully and churned butter and raised chickens, but she had always done those things. She would go on doing them after she married Eli.

But what about sterilizing scalpels and setting broken bones?

Townspeople began to drift in, moving slowly down the aisle, choosing seats, shushing children. Sage found herself watching everything, as if there were something to learn from this gathering of people. The light slanting through the windows cast a warm amber glaze over the church interior, illuminating dust motes caught in a shaft of sunshine. The air smelled warm and damp, and suddenly Sage saw everything in a different way.

She saw the looks on people's faces, in their

eyes—fathers concerned about their children, husbands reaching to their wives in silent communion, bent old men and their wrinkled partners clasping work-worn hands. There was something so…so elemental held within the four plain walls of this sanctuary. Something good. Something true.

What a gift life is. And love, as unexplainable as the origin of the universe, was what tied it all together and made sense of the mix of joy and heartache that life brought. It was…sacred, somehow.

Her father settled himself next to her, her mother swishing into the seat beside him, and then Aunt Cissy and Uncle John took places next to them. The rest of the pews filled, and then birdlike Letitia Halstead took her place at the harmonium.

At the first notes, Sage's eyes filled, blurring the scene into a wash of shapes and colors.

Eli Ramsey, in a new suit, his Adam's apple bobbing above his starched white shirt collar, waited beside Reverend Landon. When Sarah, in ivory lace, started down the aisle on her father's arm, Eli's face changed. His large brown eyes softened with a kind of reverence, as if he had seen an angel.

Sarah drifted forward, gripping a floppy bouquet of yellow roses and black-eyed Susans as if they would float away if she loosened her grasp. Her face looked…she looked…

Why am I crying? Sage wondered. *This is all so beautiful!*

Eli stepped forward, and after some words spoken low, Sarah was his. Sage wrapped her arms across her waist, laughed and cried along with the congregation as the minister made his closing remarks, raising his voice to be heard over the rain now drumming on the roof.

Her throat closed. A hollow ache bloomed under the buttons of her dress.

Scarcely aware of what she was doing, she edged past her parents and Aunt Cissy to the end of the pew, her eye on the open church door.

"Where are you going?" her aunt whispered. "It's raining outside."

"Swimming," Sage murmured in a choked voice. "I'm going swimming in the river."

Chapter Twenty-Six

Cord stepped out of the federal marshal's office and headed down the main street of Nogales toward the Senorita Saloon. His head still ached from last night's fandango with the bottle of whiskey, but he wasn't so pokered he couldn't think straight.

Or count. The thick envelope he'd stuffed inside his vest contained fifty one-hundred-dollar bills. His bounty money. Five thousand dollars, and this morning his body felt like he'd earned every one of them.

But now that he'd turned over Suarez's corpse, he was free of his obligation. Not only that, he was rich! He'd relish deciding how to spend his fortune, and he sure as hell looked forward to enjoying life again.

He strode across the wheel-rutted street,

passed the Grand Hotel, where he'd spent the night, and tramped into the saloon next door. Inside the smoky room, he slapped a greenback down on the counter.

"Here's the money I owe you, friend."

The barkeep pushed the bill back across the gritty oak surface. "Told ya it was on the house, Mr. Lawson. Pleasure to serve you."

"All of it? Jeez, I must have drunk eight or ten bucks worth of whiskey. You sure?"

"Twelve bucks, to be exact," the bartender corrected with a grin. "Sure I'm sure. Got kinda interesting the lower the bottle got."

"Interesting," Cord echoed. He wished to hell he could remember more of it. What he did recall was being warm and full of steak and beans for the first time in a week; beyond that, things got a bit blurry.

The barkeep leaned toward him. "I got two questions, Mr. Lawson. One, you got plans how to spend that pile of money? Little trip to Chihuahua, maybe? Booze? Bit of Mexican calico?"

Cord turned the suggestions over in his mind. Chihuahua was tempting; for some reason he wanted to keep moving south, as if he needed to get away from something.

Liquor? He'd had enough firewater last night

to float him off his horse, so at the moment, that didn't hold much appeal. And calico?

He couldn't work up a shred of enthusiasm for female companionship, either. "Can't say for sure, friend."

"Second question." The barkeep lowered his voice.

"Who's Sage?"

Cord jerked. "Sage? Did I mention that name?"

"You was drinkin' toasts to this feller all night. Flowery ones. I figgered you owe him some money."

The man's expression told Cord he hadn't been able to keep the smile off his face. In spite of himself, he felt his mouth widen into a grin. The mere sound of her name made his insides flip over.

"Yeah, that's right," he said quickly. "I'm in he— his debt."

Right up to his boot tops. Sage had reached deep inside him, touched something he'd kept hidden for twenty years. Underneath, he cared about people. Some people. Zack Beeler, who'd raised him. Nita.

And Sage West. Goddamn it, he'd lost his perspective on that intriguing mix of woman and physician. Lost his heart and soul right along with it.

Spending a bunch of dollars on some willing *señorita* might ease the physical ache for an hour, but it would never be enough; it was Sage he wanted. And she didn't cost a damn thing.

Oh, yes she does, a voice reminded him. Sage would cost him everything, right down to his freedom.

"You got a bank in this town?" he asked the barkeep.

"Sure 'nuf. Two blocks down, on the corner." He swiped his rag over the counter in lazy circles.

"Got a telegraph office?"

"Yep. Down at the train station."

Cord sat in silence so long the bartender finally moved away. An idea was taking root in Cord's brain. A crazy, damn-fool idea, but one he couldn't shake. It was so far-fetched he wondered if maybe he was still a bit drunk.

Or not drunk enough for what he planned to do. He caught the bartender's attention.

"Got any of that Red Eye left?"

The Thursday following Sarah and Eli Ramsey's wedding, Sage sank exhausted onto her front porch to read the latest issue of the *Wil-*

lamette Valley Voice, which Mrs. Benbow said included a writeup of the ceremony, along with birth announcements for Rafe and Ella Pokell's new baby boy and the twins born just two days ago to Cyrus and Una Gardiner. Sage had attended this birth, as well, which had kept her up all one night and half the next.

Now she rocked in her porch chair, working the kinks out of her weary frame and scanning the type before her. She found it difficult to keep her eyes open.

Mrs. Benbow swished past her front fence, stopping to tsk over Sage's overgrown roses. Sage leaned her head against the rocker slats and feigned sleep until the older woman tiptoed on past.

She didn't have the energy to spar with Mrs. Benbow this afternoon. Her shoulders and back ached from bending over Una during her contractions, and the ride back into town an hour ago had left her headachy from the heat. Then, when she dropped off the mare, Ginger, at the livery stable, she'd had to endure Arvo Ollesen's avuncular lecture about getting more sleep. *Your pretty mama, she see those circles under your eyes, she tell me not to give you a horse next time.*

Sage had escaped to Friedrich Stryker's newspaper office, asked about his sore knee and picked up a copy of the weekly newspaper.

She must have dozed off, because suddenly there was Arvo on her porch, shaking her shoulder. "Miss Sage, you vake up! It's here, down at the landing."

Sage peered at him through a haze of pain. "What is it, Arvo? Is someone ill?"

"Not ill, no!" the liveryman chortled. "Yust you come and see!"

He tugged her to her feet, propelled her along the lane behind the street that ran down to the river. She had to trot to keep up with him and, despite the ache in her temples, the sight of the burly Norwegian barreling ahead of her made her laugh. She'd never seen Arvo move that quickly; even mounted on one of his horses, the liveryman moved as slowly and deliberately as a turtle. Today he'd turned into a jackrabbit.

"Yust look!" Arvo pointed to the wooden landing. Beyond it, the sternwheel steamer *Eva* plowed away from the dock toward the center of the river.

"Look at what?" She saw nothing but the ripples made by the departing vessel lapping against the wooden platform.

"Dat!" Arvo gestured to a canvas-covered

mound at the far end of the loading dock. "Iss for you."

"Me! How do you know it's for me?"

"Cuz dat's vat the lading bill say." He pulled a wrinkled sheet of paper out of his pocket and shook it in her face. "Dr. Sage West, care of Ollesen's Livery, Russell's Landing, Oregon."

Sage stared into the liveryman's round blue eyes. "It's a horse, isn't it? Why would anyone send me—you—a horse?"

"Miss Sage—"

"By steamship?"

"But Miss—"

"You have hundreds of horses, Arvo. Good ones. And I like Ginger just fine."

"Miss… Dr.—"

"She's steady and gentle and—"

"—West, you lissen now, I tell you."

"Why is she all covered up like that?"

Arvo's mouth dropped open. "She?"

"The horse. It must be a mare. A stallion would be kicking the crate—"

"Vait, Dr. Sage. Vait yust vun minute. Iss not a mare. Or a stallion. Look!" The liveryman strode toward the canvas-draped object, lifted one corner of the cover and yanked it back.

Sage gasped. One shiny black wheel peeked out, the yellow-painted inner rim looking like a giant smile. As Arvo rolled the canvas all the way back, three more yellow smiles emerged. Four wheels and a gleaming black body.

"A buggy," Sage breathed.

"A Columbus Phaeton," Arvo added. "All the vay from Chicago."

Sage gulped. "But I don't know a soul in Chicago."

"Vas only shipped from Chicago," Arvo said. "From Sears Roebuck, the paper say."

But Sage was not listening. A buggy! A beautiful, shiny new buggy! With a leather top to keep off the sun and the rain, and plush forest-green upholstery and a Brussels carpet.

For *her*. For Dr. Sage West, the first doctor in Russell's Landing. The first *woman* doctor in three counties! Her heart swelled with pride and gratitude.

"But who sent it?"

Arvo lifted his arms in a shrug. "Someone who knows about you. And about Ollesen Livery."

Tears burned under her eyelids. "Was it Papa? Or Uncle John?"

Arvo's wide face looked blank. "Dunno, Miss Sage. Seems kinda funny either one of them vould order from fancy Chicago place when Portland iss yust up the river."

"Yes," Sage murmured.

"I go get a buggy horse and ve hitch it up."

Sage nodded, unable to take her eyes off the shiny black contraption. What a blessing it would be on scorching summer days and on wet, cold ones in the fall and winter to come.

Someone is thinking of me when I make my medical calls. Someone who recognized her value as a physician, who wanted her to be successful.

By the time Arvo returned, leading a sturdy sorrel mare and lugging the necessary tack, Sage was smoothing both hands over the gaily painted wheels and blinking back tears. *Someone believes in me, believes in what I am doing.*

Arvo hitched up the mare, handed Sage into the buggy and placed the reins in her hands. "You yust drive on home now, Miss Sage. I come by later and take to the livery. Free board I gif you, since you fix my hoof kick…" he slapped his thigh "…and dat boil on Cal's neck."

Sage looked down at the earnest, beaming face of the liveryman. "Thank you, Arvo."

She knew it was more than his bruised hip and Cal's boil; Arvo had a soft spot in his heart for her, and for her mama, as far back as she could remember. *Pretty Miss Nettie,* he called her. And he always blushed crimson in her company.

"Thank you," Sage said again. Then, scarcely able to see the road through the blur of tears, she clucked to the mare and set off toward home.

Another week passed. The temperature climbed higher with each passing day, the heat searing gardens and livestock and people alike. Old Grandpa Hedden collapsed from heatstroke while watering his wife's geraniums, and Sage spent a blistering afternoon bathing his face with witch hazel compresses and forcing salted water down his parched throat. When the old man was himself again, she calmed his distraught wife with healthy sips of medicinal brandy.

Then on Tuesday one of the Hamilton boys fell out of a tree swing and Sage drove her new buggy twelve miles out to their ranch and set his arm. When she returned, near dusk, she had to travel six miles in the other direction to prescribe a cough mixture for Trula Rondeau's chronic catarrh.

It was while driving home that night, the collar bells on the sorrel's bridle jingling faintly and the fat gold moon riding over her head like a ghostly ship, that Sage sensed something was wrong. The night air was so sweet with the scent of ripening apples and honeysuckle that she opened her mouth wide as if to taste it. An evening songbird twittered in one of the two big maple trees at the edge of town, but all at once she reined the buggy to a stop.

A sharp-edged ache filled her.

Something was missing.

The aching, desperate certainty stayed lodged in her bone marrow until Sage gave up trying to sleep. She had been without rest for a day and a half, but it made no difference; she rolled and tossed on the feather mattress in her bedroom upstairs and finally jerked to a sitting position.

She had to *do* something, but what? She'd already rolled two dozen yards of muslin bandages, boiled up another batch of horehound syrup for Mrs. Rondeau, reinspected her surgical instruments and wiped them all with alcohol for the third time that week. Aside from a call for her medical services, she had nothing to occupy her mind.

Worse, she had nothing to occupy her body, which had suddenly developed an unexpected life of its own. Her thoughts skittered, her head full of dandelion puffs. Her arms ached, her thighs ached; her belly clenched and tightened at every sound.

What on earth was wrong with her?

Nothing, a voice within her said. *This is what hunger feels like.*

Hunger! Hunger for what? Sage flopped onto her belly. She'd stuffed herself with thick slices of bread and Aunt Cissy's blackberry jelly the minute she'd arrived at the house. The bread was fresh-baked the day before, the jelly so sweet and flavorful it made her cheeks hurt. It was her favorite snack, even during medical school.

She got up, marched down the stairs to the kitchen and gobbled down two more slices with a glass of warm milk. Still she felt so restless she couldn't keep her feet still. Back and forth she paced across the kitchen floor, up the hallway, into the second parlor, back to the kitchen.

She circled the perimeter of her small bedroom, around and around on the blue braided wool rug, her toes curled into the soft fibers. For the first time, she noticed how good it felt.

And then she knew what was wrong. She was waiting for something. Waiting to hear Cord's voice, to feel his hands on her skin.

Lord in heaven, she was hungry for *him. Him!* The man who had taught her about life, and loving. About herself.

But he is not coming back.

She knew that for a certainty. When—if—he

captured Antonio Suarez, he would ride off on another chase. That's what kept a loner like Cordell Lawson going.

The thought of Cord's free and easy spirit trapped in town life even made her smile. He would never risk it. One part of him would chafe under the yoke of civilization and the social obligations that came with it.

Cord would always long to be free.

What do I do then, with this hole in my heart?
Climb back into bed and try to forget him.

Forget the pull on her senses and the fire inside that the mere thought of the man aroused.

Sage pulled the sheet up to her chin and gritted her teeth. *You wanted to be a doctor? Then* be *one!*

Chapter Twenty-Seven

The gray mare plodded south out of Nogales, heading for the Mexican state of Sonora. Cord's saddlebags bulged with provisions—coffee, dried beef, beans, and the sun-parched, hot green chilis he liked to flavor his food with when traveling south of the border.

He'd ridden this trail before, once when he'd delivered a fugitive to the authorities in Magdalena, and again when he'd rescued Nita from her drunken father. Like most trails, it was dusty and hot.

Usually he liked the hardship, even the loneliness of wending his way farther and farther from civilization, if he could call the sprinkling of faded storefronts and near-empty saloons in Nogales civilization. Today, Cord felt different in a way he couldn't quite put his finger on. Not dried out and muzzy from too much drink. Not tense and short-tempered as he'd been while tracking Antonio Suarez. Just…different. Even his horse sensed something.

The mare kept stopping to sniff at patches of greenery along the way, and Cord had to press his spurs against her hide to keep her moving forward. Each time they halted, the mare stretched her neck to look back at him, as if questioning the direction. Each time he felt the animal's skin quiver under his boot heel he regretted having to prod her forward. It was almost as if the horse had a better idea.

"Which would be what, Sugar-girl?" Cord murmured to the slow-moving animal.

The mare blew out her breath in a whoosh, put her head down and took a reluctant step forward.

"You want to stop wandering? Settle down somewhere?"

Cord's fingers tightened on the reins until his knuckles stood out. What in hell…? *What the devil made him say that?*

He drew rein smack in the middle of the trail and sat listening to his heartbeat turn ragged. Something had punched the breath right out of him.

He closed his eyes against the sun's glare,

bent his head to catch his wind. Behind his lids rose a willowy image with a jaunty purple feather stuck in her hat.

His pulse kicked. A longing he'd never known slammed him in the gut.

You don't owe me a thing, she had said.

Sure he didn't. He threw back his head and laughed out loud. He'd been roped and tied with a daisy chain so delicate he hadn't even noticed it, yet so strong he knew it would hold him forever.

He let go of the reins and stretched his arms wide. He didn't have a hole in his head; he had a big girl-shaped hole in his heart.

Whether the mare had suddenly developed a will of her own, or whether she read Cord's unconscious intent, he didn't stop to puzzle out.

Horse and rider turned north, toward Oregon.

It was the hottest, driest August Russell's Landing had ever experienced. Men on haying crews collapsed regularly, sending Sage trudging through fields of prickly stubble to pour cold, salty lemonade down throats and deliver yet another lecture about the dangers of dehydration in hot weather. The crews stubbed the toes of their boots in the parched ground while she talked and fanned the unfortunate farmhand with a stiff fan she'd fashioned out of wrapping paper from Duquette's Mercantile.

Men were a stubborn species, she huffed to Arvo when she returned the buggy to the livery stable. "Not one lick of sense and don't take kindly to advice from a woman, even if she *is* a doctor."

Arvo just nodded and unhitched the sorrel for the second time that day. "Iss not Gardiner's hay crew I vorry about, Miss Sage. Iss you. You don't stop long enough to take any kind of a meal, and what about *you,* skedaddling all over the county in this weather? How much water *you* drink today?"

Sage sighed. "Don't fuss over me, Arvo." Between Arvo and her mother she felt as coddled as a baby chick.

"Your pretty mama, she vorry, too."

"I've had half a gallon of cold water from Gardiner's spring," she assured him. And another quart of lemonade waiting in her pantry cooler. Pink, after she'd added a dab of Aunt Cissy's jelly.

True, she was bone-tired and soggy with perspiration. Her hand strayed to the top button of her wilted white waist; oh, how she longed to bare her steamy skin to the fresh air....

She fiddled with the button loop, then caught

herself when Arvo's round blue eyes widened. Well, she guessed that could wait. In polite society one didn't expose one's chest to the breeze when one was out and about.

The smile that had started at Arvo's horrified expression faded, and her heart knotted like one of the liveryman's half hitches. She missed Cord.

She would miss him for the rest of her days. *Yes, men are a stubborn species, all right.* Maddeningly impervious to the joys of…well, marriage. And in Cord's case, resistant to even the idea of permanence.

She turned away from the inquiring gaze of the stable owner and marched down the street. It was Thursday again. She'd stop by the newspaper office and pick up the latest issue of the *Willamette Valley Voice.*

The instant she turned the corner onto Main Street, she saw Mrs. Benbow sailing down the board sidewalk toward her.

"Ain't seen it yet, have ya, child?"

"Seen what?"

"Why, the newspaper, of course. The *Valley Voice.* My stars, that man has a sense of the ridiculous if you ask me."

"You mean Mr. Stryker?" Sage hid her smile. Almost every Thursday she ran into Mrs.

Benbow in town and they had the same conversation.

Nelda Benbow's gray curls bobbed. "That man," she muttered. "Every single week, it never fails. He gets the whole town into an uproar. I cannot imagine what's got into him.... The worst part of it is, the harm's done soon as the ink's dry. And the embarrassment," she added in an outraged tone. She sent Sage a sympathetic look.

"Oh? What has Mr. Stryker printed this time?"

"Now, you best set down afore you read it, Sage, honey." Mrs. Benbow patted her shoulder and barreled on down the walkway toward Duquette's Mercantile.

"Read what?" Sage murmured. More about the school board? Or was it another diatribe by Seth Duquette about rebuilding the jail and hiring a new sheriff?

She headed straight for the newspaper office.

"Why, good afternoon, Dr. West." Friedrich Stryker rose from his desk and came toward her, an odd, lopsided smile on his face. "Stopped in for your newspaper, I see."

"As I do every Thursday, Mr. Stryker. How is your knee today?"

"My knee?" The editor looked blank for an instant.

"Yes. Your sore knee," Sage reminded him.

"It…it's just fine, Sage, uh, Dr. West. Just fine." He rolled up a copy of the newspaper and secured it with a length of twine. "That's mighty effective liniment you've been bringing me. I must, er, return the favor in some way."

Sage frowned. "You've paid me for every jar of that ointment. You owe me nothing."

"Ah." The silly smile was back. "I hope you will keep that in mind, that I don't owe you anything, especially after—" The lanky editor snapped his gray-bearded jaw shut. "Here." He thrust the rolled up newspaper into her hand.

She opened her reticule, but he stopped her from reaching into it. "Keep your money, Sage. For you, this issue is free."

Free? How very odd. In all the years she'd known Friedrich Stryker he had pinched every nickel and penny until it squeaked.

Sage thanked him, spun on her heel and headed down the boardwalk toward home as fast as she could decently walk.

Something was going on. She couldn't wait to find out what it was.

Chapter Twenty-Eight

Sage swished through her front gate so fast her skirt fanned the overgrown dahlias into a row of nodding crimson faces. Up the steps she went, newspaper clutched in her hand. Rain threatened, but she didn't care. The sound of thunder suited her mood exactly.

She plopped into the porch rocker, took a moment to catch her breath, and spread the front page open on her lap.

The first glance at the bold banner headline sucked all the air out of her lungs.

MARRY ME.

What an unusual headline! And in 60 point type, too, the same size the *Voice* used for announcements of war or edicts from the president.

"Marry who?" she wondered aloud. "Who is doing the asking?"

Below the headline an article boxed in a fancy border caught her eye. New Hospital To Be Built.

New hospital! Russell's Landing didn't have even an *old* hospital.

Her eyes scanned the type. "…anonymous donor…land at the south edge of town…old McConnell homestead, near Dr. West's residence…"

"Well, of all the—" No one had told *her* anything about it.

The adjacent article was something about rebuilding the jail and hiring a new sheriff. She saw Seth Duquette's hand in this. Would that man never give up?

But her breath caught when a name jumped out at her. "The new sheriff…Cordell Lawson."

Now *that* was a piece of pure imagination on Seth's part. She'd have to speak to him in the morning.

But what a start it gave her, to think that…

Her gaze jumped to the third story on the page. Local Doctor Engaged?

Local doctor? She was the *only* doctor! And of course she was "engaged." Twenty-four hours a day she tended patients, dispensed medicines, checked on the elderly, cleaned instruments, boiled up concoctions, visited…

Unless they meant…*engaged?* As in to be married? She read further.

Residents of Russell's Landing await with interest the answer to the question posed in today's edition of the *Voice*. And that question is whether Dr. Sage West…

What on earth?

…and Cordell Lawson…

Oh! She leaped to her feet, letting the newspaper slide off her lap to the porch floor. If this was Nelda Benbow's idea of a joke, she'd strangle the woman with her bare hands!

Sage undid the top button of her blouse so she could catch her breath in the suffocating heat, then found herself skimming down the porch steps toward Mrs. Benbow's trim white house across the road.

Before she'd gone three steps past her gate, she stopped short. A tall man moved toward her, leading a gray horse.

Sage stood as frozen as a block of salt, listening to the thunder rolling across the valley. Or was that her heart?

He dropped the mare's lead and strode toward her, his long legs moving in that lazy, loose-limbed way she remembered.

"Close your mouth, Sage. A fly'll get in."

A fat raindrop splatted onto her nose. "Cord?" The word came out wobbly, as if it had been rubbed over a washboard.

He stepped close to her, so near she could see the dark stubble on his chin, smell the mixture of sweat and horse and dust that set her body trembling.

"Wh-what are you doing here?" she managed to ask over the tight feeling in her throat.

He moved in closer, until her chin brushed his open shirt collar. Lifting his hands to her neck, he began undoing the next four buttons of her blouse, spreading the white fabric open to expose her skin to the cooling air.

"Sure is hot today," he breathed.

"It's starting to rain," she said in a dazed voice. In the next instant she jerked to awareness. "Cord, stop! Think of Mrs. Benbow! She's sure to be watching."

His fingers smoothed her bare shoulders. "Yeah." He tightened his hands. "Let her watch. In a minute I'm going to kiss you, and she won't want to miss that, either.''

''She'll put something scandalous in the news—''

Sage closed her eyes. She must be hallucinating in the afternoon heat. A glass of cold lemonade would bring her out of it, but for some reason she couldn't move a single muscle. Something held her, warm and steady across her back, pulling her forward until…

When his mouth found hers, she gave herself up to the dream. *Oh, dear Lord, let me never wake up.*

Her thoughts tumbled like windblown thistles. The newspaper. The headline. *This must be real, after all.* Inexplicably, she began to cry.

She opened her eyes, touched Cord's unshaved cheek with her fingers. ''How did you…?''

''Bribed the editor,'' he said with a grin. ''Wonderful invention, the telegraph. Had to ride like hell to get here in time.''

Sage stared at him. ''In time for what?''

''To marry you. Hell's half acre, Sage, don't you read the newspaper?''

''Oh, I read it all right. Most of today's was pure tosh, fanciful stories about a new hospital, a new sher—''

"Yeah," Cord said, holding her gaze. "Thought you'd need one."

Her heart jumped. "Need one what?"

The rain began in earnest, spotting his vest, wetting her hair, her unbuttoned blouse. She watched his face through a blur of moisture, saw his grin widen and a hot light turn his eyes from soft sage into two smoldering emeralds.

"Need one hospital," he said. "Need one sheriff. At least I hope so, since I need a job." He paused and swallowed. "And I hope you need…me."

Sage stared at him, opened her mouth, closed it and put her arms around him. *Are you watching this, Mrs. Benbow? Cord Lawson has just asked me to marry him.*

She reached up, tossed his sweat-stained hat into her dahlia bed and pulled his head down to hers. She kissed him for a long, long time.

And I'm going to say yes.

"It's raining," he whispered at last against her lips.

"Yes."

"I love you, Sage. Things don't matter a damn unless we're together."

"Yes."

He turned his face up to catch the rain. "Let's go swimming in the river before the wedding."

She clung to him with all the strength she had. "Yes," she murmured. "Yes."

The ceremony took place the next evening. The air smelled sweet and clean after the rain, and the glow of candlelight washed the interior of the Methodist Church with a warm golden haze. Townspeople and farm folk crowded into the pews and listened to Letitia Halstead play Bach preludes on the harmonium.

Outside in the soft, early evening shadows, Mayor Billy West walked up and down with his daughter while she tried to calm her prewedding jitters.

"'Tain't nuthin' to be scared of, honey-girl."

Sage thought her insides would float away over the tops of the maple trees. "I'm not s-scared, Pa."

"Then stop shakin'. You already know the man physical-like, so you don't need advice on that score. If it's the 'death do us part' aspect, well, do what yer mama and I done. Jes' take it one day at a time and don't waste any of it."

"My dress...do I look all right?"

Her father held her at arm's length, his blue eyes shining. "Yer mama's been savin' that purty lace dress all these years, waitin' fer you to wear it. You look so beautiful it makes my eyes water.''

''My hair is still damp,'' Sage murmured.

''Been swimmin' again, huh? Lord, that man is a peculiar mix. Who'd want to get wet in a river when water's already pouring outta the sky?''

''He does. I do. It's…something he taught me.''

''Plumb tetched, the both of ya.'' Billy dropped a kiss onto her forehead. ''Come on, honey-girl, take my arm. I hear Miz Letitia playin' that wedding march she's so fond of.''

When they entered the church, a gasp went up from the congregation. Skirts rustled, pews squeaked as everyone stood up. Then Sage and her father took a step forward.

She looked down the aisle and saw Cord waiting for her, tall and straight-backed in a dark suit and vest. His hair was damp, too; she could tell by the unruly wave that poked up on one side. Even from here, his eyes warmed her.

She passed Mrs. Benbow, perched on the edge of the pew next to Friedrich Stryker, who surreptitiously blew his nose, while his wife, Flora, clucked beside him. Arvo and Cal Ollesen sat with Cal's wife, Ruth, between them. Arvo had never married, but his brother's two sons tumbled over him with unconscious abandon until Ruth reached over and settled them down.

There were newlyweds Sarah and Elijah Ramsey, holding hands, and Natasha Petrov, steadying her ailing husband's trembling fingers within hers. Next to them sat Joshua Duquette and his son, Seth, dry-eyed despite the death of Mrs. Duquette two weeks earlier.

Sage's mother sniffled in the first pew, next to Aunt Cissy and Uncle John and her cousin, Matt, who'd arrived on the train earlier in the day. Sage's eyes filled at the sight of them, all the people she loved here in this room.

And Cord, waiting to make her his wife.

Her father laid her hand in Cord's extended palm, coughed and stepped back to join her mother.

"Dearly beloved..."

Sage scarcely heard the minister's words. Her heart, under the ivory silk, swelled and hammered until she was sure it would burst.

"Who gives this woman into the estate of marriage?"

She heard a pew creak behind her, and then her father's voice. "Her mother, Henrietta West, and William West, her father, give this woman to be married." His voice broke on the last word.

Tears clogged her throat. She'd bet Mama had coached him.

Why am I crying? Within an hour she would belong to Cord for the rest of their days on earth. She wanted to laugh out loud, sing, throw her arms around him—around everyone—dance barefoot on the cool grass. *This is the happiest day of my life!*

"Do you, Sage Martin West, take this man..."

Within an hour they would climb the stairs to her bedroom and he would take her into his arms.

"I...yes, I do."

"Do you, Cordell James Lawson, take..."

She couldn't look at him as he slipped a gold band over her finger, and then she lifted her head and met his gaze. She couldn't see his face clearly for the tears blurring her vision.

His voice was low and calm. "I do."

Yes. Yes, yes, yes!

And then Cord surprised her. He took her hands in his and said some words that weren't in the ceremony, his steady green eyes glistening with moisture. "You have my heart, and all that I own, and all that I am. Always."

There was a moment of stunned surprise, and

in that silence he kissed her, his mouth warm and gentle on hers.

"I love you," he whispered against her temple.

And then it was over.

Or perhaps, Sage thought as they walked hand in hand down the aisle, perhaps it was just beginning.

Epilogue

September 1, 1884

Sunday evening at the Methodist Church, Sage Martin West, of Russell's Landing, Douglas County, was joined in marriage to Cordell James Lawson, lately of Arizona. The bride wore her mother's wedding gown of ivory peau de soie fashioned with a wide sash and deeply flounced hem ruffle.

The bride was given away by her father, Mayor William Martin West. Attending the ceremony from St. Louis was Mr. Matthew Montgomery, the bride's cousin.

After the ceremony, the couple departed on an extended wedding journey into the Bear Mountain Wilderness.

Upon their return, Mr. Lawson will take up his duties as the new sheriff of Russell's Landing, while his wife will resume her medical practice on Maple Falls Road, where the couple will reside.

June 17, 1885

Born to Dr. Sage West Lawson and Sheriff Cordell Lawson, a daughter, on June 15. Christened Constance Henrietta, the baby has the honor of being the first child born at the new Lawson-West Hospital on Maple Falls Road.

* * * * *

If you loved HIGH COUNTRY HERO,
be sure to look for Lynna Banning's
next Harlequin Historical coming
in Fall 2004!

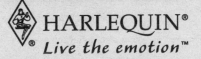

IN THE PRIM-AND-PROPER PHILADELPHIA OF 1820, COMES A SHOCKING MARRIAGE....

Wealthy Philadelphia widower Justin Randolph does not want a wife, he simply needs one, to provide a mother for his young children.

For Elizabeth Frasier, who is mistaken for Justin's mail-order bride, marriage to the handsome stranger presents an escape from the unwanted attentions of wealthy and abusive Reginald Burton-Smythe.

Both enter this marriage of convenience with no intention of falling in love, but God has a different plan altogether....

Steeple Hill®

Available in June 2004.

www.steeplehill.com

SDC515